THE NOVICE
WAYFINDERS BOOK 1

C.A. MORLEY

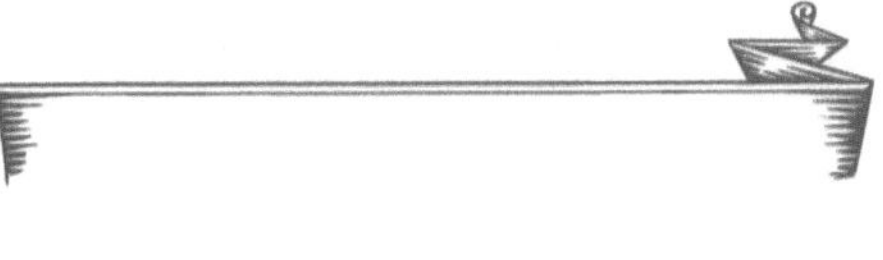

All Rights Reserved

ISBN: 979-8-9870797-0-6
Published by C.A. Morley
www.camorleyauthor.com

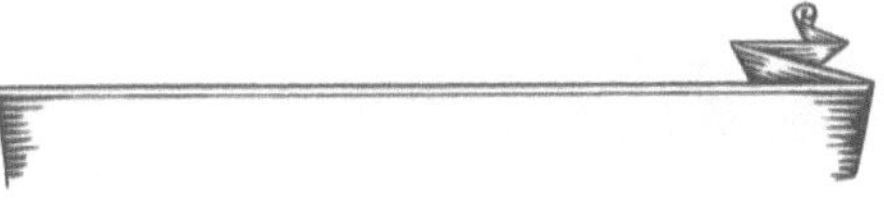

Acknowledgements

I WISH TO THANK THOSE who helped make this book possible:

My daughter, Samantha, for the fabulous Cover Art, Map, Logo, and Headers.

My husband for encouraging me to pursue writing fiction and his willingness to listen whenever I needed a sounding board.

Vivian, my Alpha Reader extraordinaire, who made my ideas even better, helped with editing, and gave expert advice on all things medieval.

My CheerReaders, Beba, Nic, and Laura, for their input and encouragement. Also, Beba and Nic for their help with some proofreading and Laura for her help with some editing.

Author C.S. Johnson for giving my book a blurb that does my story justice.

And, everyone else who contributed in some way.

MAP

NORTH SEA
LIVANIA
FULSAN
DYLARI
KILNAR
BARINY
TANDOLA
KARPYDOSA
MALTANY
CORITHANE
PENTHIA
BAIONI
THAYNI
CALANDORE
ZINDO
SOUTH SEA
ELNORE
PASSAVO
YALAMAR
SALOVA
KOSHBA
PALM ISLANDS

Chapter 1
Disturbing Dreams

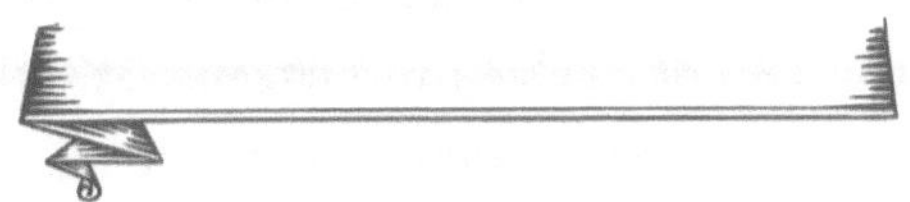

AMITY LAY ON HER BACK and watched her warm breath puff into the cold morning air. She was glad for the double layer of heavy wool blankets and woolen flannel sheets tucked snugly around her neck. Sometimes upon awakening in the night, she would pinch herself to make sure she wasn't dreaming, but in the morning, as soon as she experienced the shock of her bare feet hitting the cold stone floor, Amity knew she wasn't.

It was the middle of winter, the first month of a brand new year, following the excitement of the Midwinter Festival and Amity's very first week as a novice priestess of Riaas the Watcher. She was thrilled to have been selected and looked forward to everything she would learn during her training. Housing and lessons were in the monastery built next to the Temple of Riaas in the City of Tilmar. Her room was on the first floor in the female wing of the building for novices. On the ground floor were unmarried priestesses.

Amity no longer had to share a big bed with her two older sisters. Now she had her own bed in a small room she shared with another novice. Felicia, who was already a year into her novitiate, made sure to remind Amity, whenever they were in their room together, that she was one year older and, therefore, had to be obeyed. Thankfully, the girls spent a good portion of that time sleeping, so Amity could manage. At least she didn't have someone breathing in her face or complaining about her cold feet all night. And she didn't have to worry about anyone stealing the blankets, then blaming her and calling her a "blanket hog," complete with oinking noises. It was her oldest sister, Esme, who was the blanket hog! Well, mostly, anyway. But none of that really mattered now that Amity was on the path to seeing her dream come true. What she wanted, more than anything in the world, was to become one of the ordained, a fully-fledged priestess of Riaas the Watcher.

As Amity dressed quickly in the crisp air, she thought about everything that had happened to bring her to this momentous point in her life. She had been one of the few chosen last autumn to become a novice priestess of Riaas. Each year, Servants of Riaas would interview young boys and girls interested in joining the order in Livania's three cities and the larger towns in the kingdom. Any child between the ages of twelve to fourteen was welcome to apply. The smaller towns scattered through the countryside were placed on rotation, to be visited only once every few good years, and last autumn had been the turn of Amity's town. She had been twelve at the time of the interview, and, not long after, she turned thirteen, just before Midwinter.

It had been a sunny day when children from Amity's school had lined up outside four classrooms, with two rows of boys and two rows of girls. Inside the classrooms, priests and priestesses of Riaas were asking each child questions.

The number of fellow students who had lined up shocked Amity. What were they all doing there? It wasn't fair that all these children had come when she knew most of them hadn't shown any scrap of interest in the teachings of Riaas before that day!

All the unexpected competition and the long wait to speak to a priestess made her stomach churn. Joining the priesthood had been Amity's dream since she had been ten, when she'd first felt the call. Unlike so many of her classmates and friends, she'd been determined in her ambition. They hadn't seemed to be very serious, and changed their minds almost weekly about what they wanted to do "when they grew up."

Amity was a wreck at the start of her interview. Her mouth was so dry that swallowing and speaking was a struggle. Afraid she might give the wrong answer to any questions, she could barely answer at all. The white-robed priestess smiled kindly, touched Amity's hand, and, nodding to her yellow-robed clerk, suggested that Amity take a moment to compose herself. The clerk wrinkled her brow, seemingly frustrated at the delay, but still handed Amity a cup of water, which she drank deeply, nearly choking as it went down the wrong way.

Once Amity's brief flurry of coughing and nose blowing were over, they resumed the interview. The priestess sat back, steepled her fingers, and encouraged Amity to tell her why she wished to become a priestess of Riaas. Remembering her wonderful visit to the temple made Amity forget to be self-conscious about her mishap when drinking the water. She had relived that experience so many times in the last two years that it wasn't at all hard for her to describe the whole thing.

Amity shared what she'd seen and experienced. It had been a beautiful sunny day when she saw the temple for the first time. All that white marble sparkled in the sunlight, and it was breathtaking. The gleaming white continued inside the temple with the marble floors, curved arches, carved columns, and the spotless white robes worn by the priests and priestesses.

It was fascinating, watching the priests and priestesses move so gracefully as they guided people to the Pool of Blessing beneath the statue of Riaas. The huge stone god sat on the edge of the pool, his feet in the clear water that flowed silently past his calves. Even from where Amity stood at a distance, the god had seemed formidable. She felt tingly all over, looking up at him.

Amity stood in line, holding Papa's hand while clutching the copper coin he had given her in the other. She felt safe holding his large calloused hand with her small one as she tried to see everything at once. Her two older sisters walked closely beside Mama in her best gown and Amity's favorite shade of blue. When it was their family's turn to join the front line of supplicants at the pool, it felt as if Riaas was looking straight at Amity with his golden eyes, and she was transfixed.

A few of the ordained stood just beyond the pool, quietly talking to visitors. Amity's father explained in a low voice that she should throw her coin into the pool as an offering, then pray for a blessing and guidance from the god. She watched other people doing the same until it was her turn. Sometimes a priest or priestess would take a person to the side, giving them a word right away. The other visitors went to wait in the courtyards on the left and right to receive their word, if there was to be one. Not everyone was so blessed.

Papa gave her a nudge to keep moving. So many people were at the temple, and the line to the pool was long. Not wanting to miss her opportunity, Amity said a heartfelt prayer and threw her coin in with zeal. Afterwards, her sisters made fun of her for doing it the wrong way around, but Amity decided it didn't matter what they said because in that moment, she had felt her heart soar, and a desire had stirred in her belly to join the priesthood. From that day on, she'd become determined about the priesthood.

Once Amity had finished telling her story, the priestess thanked her and told her the interview was over. Amity's eyes grew wide with surprise. "But, what about the questions?"

"The questions are not so important. It was your story that I wanted to hear. Do not worry, little one. You told it well." The smile of the priestess was the last thing Amity saw before the yellow-robed clerk impatiently shoved her out the door.

Later that same evening, the priestess paid Amity and her family a visit, handing them the formal gold and white scroll – the official invitation for Amity to come to Tilmar in the New Year. Only two children from their town had been chosen, one girl and one boy. While her parents had some reservations about their daughter leaving home at such a young age, Amity was thrilled and couldn't wait for her departure day.

People traveled to Livania to receive healing or guidance. There were many places where one could go for healing, and most of these businesses were in Livania's three cities. In the City of Tilmar, there were at least thirty different places to choose from. But, if you wanted supernatural guidance, there was only one place in all of Livania.

As Amity straightened her clothes, she admired the winter uniform. It enhanced that feeling of belonging to something significant. She sat back down on the bed to pull up her woolen stockings. She was getting better at the morning routine and didn't need to concentrate so hard on getting everything right.

In the few days since she had arrived at the monastery, Amity hadn't had a chance to feel homesick. Of course, she missed her parents, her sisters, and the familiar comfort of their small home and everyday routines, but all that paled in comparison to her excitement at actually being here.

The most important part of their early training, and one of the first things taught, was to develop their skills as listeners. She had already learned that Riaas used different methods to speak to his servants and that they must listen not only with their ears but also with their hearts and minds. Sometimes he would speak through a dream, a thought, or a vision. If a novice believed they had received a word from him, they had to share it with one of the ordained. Then the priest or priestess would help them confirm the word before passing it on to the person for whom it was intended.

Amity had just finished braiding her hair when she blinked in surprise. Felicia, who had been peacefully sleeping moments before, was suddenly fully dressed and putting on her slippers. "Wow, you're fast!"

Like Amity, Felicia was wearing the novice's winter uniform. Underneath a blue woolen ankle-length dress with a darker blue shawl for extra warmth were a linen shift, drawstring drawers, woolen petticoat, and woolen stockings. The uniform might be considered a great equalizer for two novices from totally different backgrounds, except that Felicia, coming from a well-to-do family in the city, still managed to put on airs, treating Amity like a backward country girl.

Felicia gave a final tug to her long auburn braid and headed for the door. Looking back over her shoulder, she sniffed, "And you've been standing there daydreaming. Anyway, it's too cold to dally. I'm heading to the privy. Make sure there's fresh wash water by the time I get back."

Amity narrowed her eyes at Felicia's retreating form until the door shut with a firm and somehow very Felicia-like click. Fetching wash water every morning was one of the daily tasks allocated to her by Felicia, who Amity had discovered was a little bit of a bossy-boots. Amity had begun calling her "Princess Fee Fee." But only in her head.

Amity knotted her braid tie and picked up a small silver-framed hand glass. It was new, a traditional thirteenth birthday gift from her mama. As she checked to be sure her thick ash-brown hair was tied in a smooth and even braid, she was reminded, once again, of just how much she looked like her papa. She had inherited not only his hair and plain grey eyes but also his rangy build, broad shoulders, and calm demeanor. His thirteenth birthday gift to her had also been the traditional silver but in the down-to-earth form of the thirteen silver coins usually given to boys. "To grow your fortune on," he'd said. But they'd been polished to a fare-thee-well and presented in a beautiful, totally impractical little silver brocade purse that had completely charmed her practical little soul.

Having experienced a rapid growth spurt the previous summer, Amity was now taller than her sisters even though they were older by four and six years. But then, she mused, unlike her, they were both exact copies of their dainty mama, right down to their honey-blonde locks, delicate bone structures, and changeable blue eyes. When the three of them walked down the street together, her sisters attracted a great deal of admiration from others. Sometimes people put in the effort to say a few polite words to Amity, but mostly she went unnoticed. And now Esme was even to be married at Midsummer. Amity was really hoping to be allowed time off to attend the wedding.

Grabbing the water pail, Amity dashed out the door to fetch water from the well before going to the privy herself. Figuring how late it was, at least there wouldn't be a wait-line at the privies.

Afterwards, she quickly washed her hands and face before donning her short dark-blue cloak and running down the stairs to breakfast. Amity's heart was pounding by the time she reached the large garden courtyard and joined a few others in their colored robes as they hurriedly walked along the peristyle toward breakfast. There were several other novices dressed in blue, three older girls dressed in the yellow of more advanced novices, and even one tall priest hurrying along in his flowing white robes.

The central section of the main building ahead held the dining hall in the middle, with classrooms and offices on either side. Amity enjoyed the extra learning she received at the monastery. Along with the usual math and calligraphy studies, she was also learning about other races, their cultures and customs, and Emirlinn, the common tongue, as many foreigners were coming to Livania to receive a word from Riaas.

Similar to the rest of the monastery, the main building was made of stone with a ground floor and first floor. Behind the dining hall were the kitchens, laundry, and stillrooms. She hadn't yet been assigned any work duties in that section, but Amity and all the other new arrivals had received a tour of the property. Having a general idea of where everything was, was helpful. Her slow start this morning caused her to be almost last in line to enter the dining hall behind the tall priest.

The dining hall was where the entire community of novices and ordained gathered for meals and important meetings. Upon entering, the first indication that something wasn't right was the complete silence in the room. A somber atmosphere had replaced the usual cheery hum of chatter punctuated by the clinks of cutlery and dishes. She wondered uneasily if someone important had died.

Amity quickly joined the other young women and girls in blue, seated at their designated tables. Felicia was already there, comfortably hemmed in by her friends. Amity was still too new to have made any particular friends, so she found a vacant spot on the opposite bench. She had been looking forward to breaking her fast as she was very hungry, but then she realized there was no food on the tables. Now that was also strange. The others would usually be eating toasted bread and hot cereal with honey by now.

Looking around at everyone's faces, Amity tried to figure out what was happening. Some of the girls at her table, as well as people at other tables, had their heads bowed, possibly praying. A few were even crying. What had shattered their peaceful morning?

Amity caught the eye of an older girl across from her. Was her name Eva? Amity decided not to use it in case she was wrong. Leaning forward, she asked softly, "What's going on?"

Shrugging, the girl tipped her head and whispered, "We have been told not to speculate until High Priest Dante and High Priestess Celeste speak to us."

Amity's eyes grew wide. What kind of an answer was that? Even though she was disappointed, she still did the agreeable thing and "mm-hmmed" quietly in her throat.

To Amity's relief, the girl sitting next to her leaned closer and chimed in. She whispered, "All we know is several novices and ordained received disturbing dreams from Riaas last night."

Precisely at that moment, a priestess walked past and gave them a stern look. Amity and the other girl quickly looked down, and none dared speak again.

Amity glanced surreptitiously at the young male novices sitting a few tables away. She had never been interested in the silly boys she knew at home, but there was one boy here at the monastery who had caught her attention. It was impossible not to notice him. He was handsome, well-mannered, and stood taller than the other boys his age. He was obviously a favorite among his peers and with everyone else too.

When Amity had asked the girl sitting next to her at supper two nights ago about him, the girl had dramatically sighed and clutched her heart. "Paxton," she said, "is fifteen, the grandson of Dante and Celeste, and everyone expects him to become high priest someday." She'd also told Amity that he "is completely dreamy, sweet as pie, and all the girls are hopeful he'll give them a second look." Sighing again, the girl had turned back to her dinner, drawing a heart in her mashed potatoes while leaving Amity sitting there feeling nonplussed.

Whenever Paxton was in the same room, Amity was a little embarrassed to admit she watched him. She couldn't help noticing his thick curly dark hair and blue eyes, and she loved it when he smiled, showing even white teeth. He smiled quite frequently, although never directed at her. There were plenty of pretty girls here, and a lot of them would walk by and smile at Paxton and his friends. *If I was more like one of my sisters, I might have a chance, but I might as well wish for the moon. I'd be more likely to get it.*

Observing Paxton's troubled expression, Amity snapped back to the present, remembering there were other things more important to be thinking about right now. She pulled her braid forward, nervously pulling on it as her stomach began clenching with worry. All this waiting and not knowing how long until they heard something was unsettling. Also, no one had told her what she was supposed to be doing while they waited. *Perhaps I should practice my prayers to Riaas.*

As Amity silently said her prayers, she heard the chime of bells from the front of the room. Everyone turned and looked up to where the head table stood on a long low dais. People began to whisper to one another as High Priest Dante and High Priestess Celeste entered, their shoulders stiff and their hands folded in front of them. They were married and, though they were in their seventies, usually appeared younger and livelier than their ages. Both were tall and slim, with silver-white hair and the same blue eyes they had passed down to Paxton. Celeste had her hair piled up on her head, and Amity briefly wondered how she got it to stay. She'd met the couple at her official welcome. But, other than that, she'd only seen them at a distance. She wondered what it was like for Paxton to have them for grandparents. Today they looked older with pinched faces and worry lines around their eyes. Once they came to a halt in front of the head table, the room went completely still.

Celeste nodded at Dante. He took a deep breath, gestured to the room, and began speaking in his deep rumbling voice, "Our dear brothers and sisters, as you know, some of you came to us in the night and this morning after experiencing disturbing dreams that seemed, without a doubt, to be portents.

Celeste and I have also received similar visions and dreams in the past two days. We have spent hours discussing how to handle these latest foretellings, and, above all else, we have been seeking out Riaas for guidance. At this time, we are going to ask that no one speaks of their dreams or visions except to senior clergy or us. Please do not discuss them or speculate amongst yourselves. We have the younger novices and the children to consider and do not want to alarm any of them unnecessarily. That having been said, we will begin to prepare for what is to come. And we will keep you fully informed through your regular meetings in your prayer groups. For now, we ask that you carry on as if nothing has changed."

A murmur of fearful questions and complaints arose from the assembly. Celeste motioned to the group with her hands and spoke in her clear voice. "Everyone, please be calm. Trust us to decide what is best. This new situation must be handled delicately. Let me remind you now of your vows. Each of you makes a promise to keep and honor them when entering as a novice, and each of you repeats and swears to them as solemn vows when ordained. Tell me now, what are your vows?"

The assembly stood, and replied in unison, "I will serve Riaas the Watcher with my whole heart. I will listen not just with my ears, but also with my heart and my mind, and allow him to speak to me. I will be trustworthy with his words. I will respect each word he gives, even if it seems trivial. I will respect the privacy of others and guard my mouth. I will seek to serve instead of being served."

Nodding, Celeste continued, "For everyone's safety, we ask that you do not speak of this situation to anyone. Remember, we cannot change even one word of a foretelling; we can only prepare for it. That is what we will be doing over these next few weeks, but we will do it discreetly."

Celeste rang a bell, and breakfast, carried in pots and on platters, was served. Amity's mouth watered, smelling the toast and sausages as she accepted a bowlful of honeyed porridge. Her stomach growled loudly, and the girl beside her giggled. The unsettled feelings brought on by this morning's strange events wore off as she ate, and soon things seemed almost back to normal as she and the other girls chatted about the day's upcoming classes and the hopes that they might visit the temple soon.

Chapter 2
Impressive Image

KING ARLO WAS A HANDSOME man, and he knew it.

Even now in his forties Arlo remained fairly fit. A slight softening at the waist and a certain breathlessness when climbing stairs were the only indicators that he wasn't as free to spend his time in physical pursuits as when he was a young heir. Kings were, after all, busy men.

He found the incipient belly to be a sting to his vanity, an annoyance as he examined his reflection. The looking glass here at the inn wasn't as big or clear as his personal one at the castle, but it would do.

Having arrived on horseback with his party the day before, the king was, of course, staying at the best and largest inn in Tilmar. The Striking Falcon was a sprawling establishment and served a very elite clientele. Six of his royal guards had taken the two adjacent rooms. He and his men had their horses stabled below. The rest of his men with their horses were in a humbler establishment down the road.

Arlo had an angular face with high cheekbones, a neatly trimmed mustache, and a short pointy beard, enhancing his sharp features. His still thick hair curling to his shoulders was silvering at his age, especially around his face. His youthful black hair had made him appear rather spirit-like but had been quite striking, as most Livanians were blue-eyed with blonde hair. He'd enjoyed standing out in the crowd, just as his own father had in his time, but nowadays, the lighter coloring of his hair was better suited to his pale grey eyes, black lashes, and very fair skin. In fact, he rather fancied that his eyes now looked like polished silver.

Thinking of his relationship with his father reminded him of his son Edson, who was now nineteen. Edson had trained as a fighter, but he was no match for his father. It seemed that the boy preferred reading to fighting! Arlo snorted; the boy was far too soft, in his opinion. Arlo had only been a few years older than Edson was now when the crown passed to him. And although he didn't plan on leaving this world anytime soon, when he did, he hoped his son would uphold his legacy.

The king remembered how it was being the heir. It had chafed, always having to be perfectly poised, and though he had had much more free time then, he still hadn't been able to go out and have fun with a group of friends as other young men could. He'd had a lot of pent-up anger in his younger years and put that aggression to use in the drill yard, where he trained hard with weapons and hand-to-hand combat. It had paid off. He had cut quite a figure back in the day.

Going forward, Arlo resolved to carve out more time in the drill yard, and perhaps eschew second helpings of... well, everything. At least for the time being. The recent feasting that was always a part of celebrating Midwinter hadn't helped.

His new manservant was turning out to be excellent. Silas had searched for and found a replacement when the shaking in his old hands could no longer be controlled. Arlo was glad he'd accepted his recommendation. Roger had been with him for just over a month now and he was already proving his worth. Not having Silas around still seemed strange at times. But then, he had had the position since Arlo's father was king, so he must be absolutely ancient by now.

Roger was a magician with a needle and the man had an unerring eye for style and color. Dressed all in black, with Roger's adjustments, including the addition of a plate to lengthen his belt, Arlo was impressed with himself. He looked broad-shouldered, trim, and confident. *Excellent!* The last thing he wanted was for gossip to float around the court that he was getting fat or perhaps becoming soft.

Roger, by doing some very fast-talking, had convinced Arlo to have a deep crimson wool plush surcoat made in the new fashion with the addition of black wolf fur on the wide lapels. Wearing it made him appear a giant among men. *Especially if I place my hands on my hips just so... Yes, I must remember to stand exactly like this.*

Today was an important day. The king had to look powerful, strong, and in control. For this reason, even though he was a tall man, Arlo still wore thick-soled boots to add to his height. As he walked down the broad front staircase of the inn, he hoped his six elite guards remembered to swap their hobnailed boots for their indoor ones. Arlo didn't want to have a repeat of five or six years back when one of his men embarrassed himself, his unit leader, and his king by slipping on the marble tiles inside the temple. That guard had been given the lowly task of training recruits for six months as punishment. Most recruits were young farm lads who barely knew which end of a sword to hold on to, and which end to poke with.

Striding out the front door of the Striking Falcon with his six guards, Arlo met the rest of his men on horseback in the circular courtyard. He stepped up to his tall black stallion and swung into the saddle. Darkness, his favorite mount, was a little skittish but soon settled down under his expert hand. His elite guards wasted no time in mounting and getting into position. Soon they were all trotting out of the inn's front gate, pushing through the crowd of commoners already gathered there.

Every year the king rode to the City of Tilmar to receive the word of Riaas. Of course, the road leading to the temple was always thronged with people shouting and waving, hoping to catch a glance from the king. And hearing them all cheer as he rode past made the effort of looking his best worth it.

Like all Livanians, Arlo knew that the word of Riaas always came to pass; perhaps not in the way one thought it would, but it always, one way or another, happened. He would accept each year's foretelling, whether good or not, and prepare accordingly. Often it had been something good, something he wanted to hear, like the year he heard that his firstborn was to be a son. Another time, he'd been warned that the barley crop would fail. During his reign, he had never experienced hearing something severely disappointing. But sooner or later, a first time for that was bound to be. The thought made Arlo frown, and he urged Darkness to a faster pace.

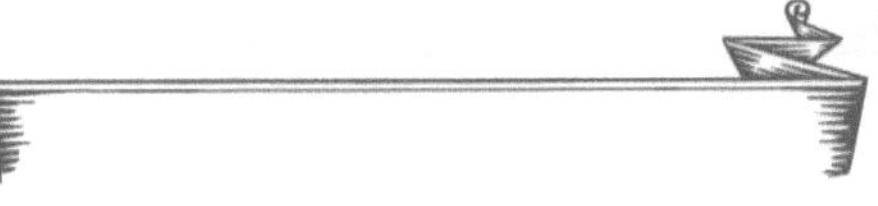

Chapter 3
Wary Watcher

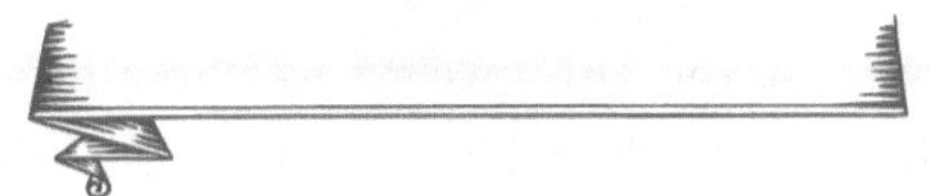

PAXTON HAD GROWN UP at the monastery, and the temple was like an extension of his home. He knew almost everything that went on in both places. From a young age, he had shown an aptitude for hearing the voice of Riaas. His grandparents were the high priest and priestess, and his parents were also ordained, so his training for a leadership role began early. Many in the priesthood believed he might be the future high priest.

Riaas the Watcher had always been his god. He didn't know anything else apart from a life dedicated to the service of Riaas. Normally, that suited him fine. But with the latest dreams, he wasn't so sure. The cost of following Riaas seemed too high. The people he loved and the life he knew were now at stake. It's what motivated him to steal a yellow robe and sneak into the temple. He tried timing the king's visit just right, so he would have less chance of being discovered. It helped that he was tall with broadening shoulders. As long as no one got a good look at his face, he could easily pass as one of the older male novices.

Temple guards were on duty every day at the entrance, controlling the number of visitors, but on the day of the king's visit, a tripling of the guard was always needed. Just thinking about the king made Paxton angry. What right did the king have to play at being a god? He was too ambitious and so sure of himself, eager to further his reach. If the king was slower to action, perhaps the upcoming events could be avoided.

Paxton paced with tense muscles. He was careful to keep his head down to avoid being recognized. A commotion at the entrance drew his attention, and he sucked in a breath as he saw what had caused it. The king had arrived. All Paxton could do was watch. It was up to his grandparents to advise the king on what Riaas had shown them. Paxton had been trained his whole life to keep silent when it wasn't his place to speak. But today, that training brought him agony.

King Arlo cut a striking figure, dressed in all his finery, as he stood under the portico at the temple's grand entrance. He was in his late forties, tall and well-built, with a slight bulge around his middle. His salt and pepper hair gave his age away. Paxton begrudgingly had to admit that the king was handsome. His grandparents were at the entrance to welcome him inside. The king's garments of crimson red and deep black contrasted against all the temple's white. Paxton shivered with a dreadful premonition. The king's red surcoat reminded him of blood, while his grandparents' white robes reminded him of purity and all that was good in the world.

His grandparents guided the king to the Pool of Blessing beneath the statue of Riaas the Watcher. Even though the king knew the way, tradition and ceremony required the high priest and priestess to accompany him. They glided silently on either side of him, wearing their temple slippers beneath long robes.

The loud clomping of the king and his men's leather boots made Paxton flinch. Six impressive royal guards had accompanied him inside. They wore dark-grey uniforms with a fabric baldric draped over their shoulders depicting the kings' heraldic badge of a black snarling long-toothed wolf's head with yellow eyes against a crimson background.

If Paxton hadn't considered this a hostile visit, he would have enjoyed watching the royal guards. Three walked in front and three behind the king, exuding aggression and armed with matching swords and daggers with silver hilts and opalescent glass jewels set in the pommels. Each held a short hardwood mace, just over a foot long and, as they walked, they watched for any threats. If people didn't clear out of the way fast enough, they would get jabbed hard with the mace. Most were quick to move out of the way, allowing the king a clear path to the Pool of Blessing. As custom demanded, the people bowed deeply or curtsied, remaining that way until after the king passed them.

Standing near the Pool of Blessing, Paxton was one of the last who needed to bow, getting a clear view of the large white opal stone hanging from a gold chain around the king's neck. The opal was a venerable icon, honoring the healing gift uniquely bestowed on some Livanians. Those born with the gift had eyes like opals. The gemstone glittered with vibrant colors, so beautiful that Paxton almost forgot to bow in time. He covered his mistake by snapping into the proper position. He certainly didn't want to raise the ire of the king's guards.

As soon as King Arlo was standing by the Pool of Blessing, Paxton shuffled a bit closer. His grandparents were waiting quietly beside the king, clutching their hands in front of them. They were so focused on him that they didn't see Paxton standing to the side. His grandfather had a bead of sweat trickling down his brow, and his grandmother's eyes were twitching. King Arlo was oblivious to their anxiety, and that made Paxton mad.

Everyone, apart from the king and his guards, was ushered out, including Paxton. He wanted to stay and listen to the word that would change everything, but he knew there was no use trying. His grandparents would honor Riaas' word no matter what.

Chapter 4
Fateful Foretelling

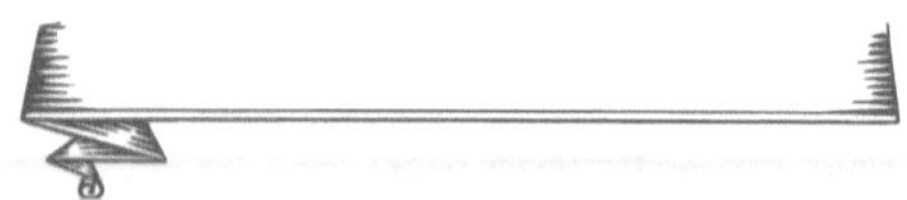

IT WAS ONLY AFTER THE Midwinter Celebrations that King Arlo would make his way to the Temple of Riaas in Tilmar each New Year. His desire for big things had been steadily growing, and today, he strongly hoped for some good news.

Upon entering the temple, High Priest Dante and High Priestess Celeste met him. They accompanied him as he purposefully strode toward the front. He came to an assertive halt at the Pool of Blessing. On the other side of the pool was the great marble statue of Riaas the Watcher. The god was seated on his throne with his feet planted in the water, facing the king.

Arlo looked up at Riaas. The god permanently held a slight forward lean as if looking straight at him. Arlo could identify with the god's kingly pose and the responsibility that came with it. He always thought it was uncanny how the golden yellow vein through the eyes made them seem alive and watching.

Pouring a pouch of gold coins into the pool, King Arlo offered a regal prayer of supplication. Then he turned to the priest and priestess expectantly. "What word do you have for me?"

Dante's neck muscle twitched, and he swallowed hard, his throat bobbing. The priest seemed to be taking his sweet time. Arlo resisted rolling his eyes.

It was Celeste who finally spoke after clearing her throat. "Livania and Karpydosa will one day form a strong alliance." She bowed and then added, "Riaas has spoken."

The king gave a tight grin. The word was short and to the point. It seemed like a lot of effort coming for something that took less than a minute. Well, truth be told, he didn't really mind. In fact, it was just what he wanted to hear. "If that is all, then I will be on my way."

Dante leaned slightly forward. Lowering his voice, he said, "May I remind you, My King, not to be too hasty."

Arlo's jaw clenched, and his hands fisted. "You forget to whom you are speaking!"

Dante cast his eyes downward. "Forgive me. I only ask that you heed the words given in the past, even to previous kings."

"Of course! Is that all?"

Dante lifted his eyes back to the king. "That is everything. Riaas has spoken."

Arlo gave a dismissive wave of his hand. "Yes, yes. I know."

IT WAS THE START OF spring when King Arlo looked over the map on the elegant wooden desk in his chambers. An urgent letter with the Karpydosa's royal seal lay open beside it from King Marin himself.

The map showed Arlo what he already knew. Karpydosa was the only country on this side of the Whistling Mountains directly situated on the South Sea, and Arlo envied Marin for that. Livania, on the other hand, had the ocean to their west beyond the Azure Mountains and the cliffs. Between Livania and Karpydosa was the Bay of Brothers. It was the only easy access point to the ocean, offering several fishing villages and one good-sized port for a few Livanian ships. But it wasn't enough. The king frowned, growling his frustration under his breath.

A shout accompanied by a loud crashing noise shook Arlo from his thoughts. Now that it was springtime, the building project was finally underway. He'd begun the plans last year, finalizing things during the winter months. Usually, the sound of construction gave him satisfaction, but being constantly surrounded by noise did sometimes rankle. It was a big project and would take time to complete. The designs were for a new extension, the royal wing, complete with a private solar and living accommodations for the royal family.

At present, his cherry wood desk was in his sitting room. It was not ideal. Arlo had told his architects to create a separate private study adjacent to his future bedchamber. Once completed, he'd be able to reach it via the bedchamber or the shared balcony. A king of his standing needed a balcony. None of the other rooms in the royal wing were getting one.

Thinking about the improvements that he was making on a humble castle made Arlo frown. His grandfather had been a true believer of Riaas, and he hadn't spared any coin on the temple in Tilmar. When his father decided to build their new castle home against the rock-face of the Azure Mountains, there wasn't enough money for things like marble from Corithane. The temple got all of it. Lately, the Royal Treasury was doing well with money pouring in from taxes. An increase of foreign visitors made up a good portion of it, from toll roads and bridges to money spent at healers and other places of business.

Arlo turned his thoughts back to the map. His eyes traced a path from Livania, past the Bay of Brothers, to Karpydosa and the South Sea below it. His latest endeavor was to gain a share in Karpydosa's lucrative shipping industry. Livania was already supplying wood at a fair price. In exchange, their kingdom received a reduction in tax for using the trade route through Karpydosa. But Bariny had a similar deal with their neighbor.

Arlo straightened and clenched his fists. He wanted to gain an edge. Something Livania had that Bariny didn't were people with the ability to heal others. The healing business was growing, and so were their cities, of which Livania now boasted of three despite being a relatively small kingdom.

Arlo's great-grandfather once made a pilgrimage to the Temple of Riaas in Penthia before his grandfather had built the one in Tilmar. He had received word from the priests in Penthia that Livanian healers were not to travel outside their borders for safety reasons. Keeping the healers inside the country had been good advice, as the healing business was now thriving, bringing in many foreigners. They all needed food and drink, places to sleep, and stables for their horses. Some came with their families, and others came with goods to trade and sell. And in the last three decades, the number of foreigners entering Livania had tripled. Yes, things were going well for the kingdom.

The king looked over at the letter once more. He didn't need to unfold the pages to know what was inside. He had already read it thrice. Prince Jurem needed a healer. He was too sick to travel, and his condition was worsening.

Lips quirking into a smile, Arlo decided to act on the word he'd received nearly three months ago. He knew who he wanted to send. His own son, Prince Edson, had the gift. It would serve his purposes if Marin were indebted to him.

Marin's son was twenty, only one year older than Edson. A friendship between the two crown princes could prove favorable in the future. And, if Edson healed Jurem, perhaps it could pave the way to secure a marriage alliance between Edson and one of Jurem's sisters or Edson's sister and Jurem. Arlo's daughter, Anwen, was beautiful and, at age seventeen, old enough to wed.

King Arlo tapped the letter against the map near Karpydosa's ports. The idea of ships with Livanian flags alongside Karpydosan ones was now within his grasp. His smile grew as he envisioned a bright future for Livania.

Chapter 5
Rising Resentment

PAXTON WAS TRYING HARD to hold back the tears of anger and frustration. His grandparents were giving final instructions to the rest of the ordained, gathered in one of the classrooms in the main building.

After the king's visit, Paxton and the other novices had been helping the ordained with preparations to travel to the Temple of Riaas in the Kingdom of Penthia. The thing that upset him the most was that his grandparents would not be joining them. Anyone willing to stay behind and face the king's wrath was most probably going to die. The dreams had shown them this.

"You will need to cross the border in smaller groups over several days, so as to not raise suspicion. It's going to be a long journey and I don't think there is enough coin to sustain you all. That is why you must also take all of the gold and silver artifacts you can carry. Sell what you need to along the way." At this, one of the ordained objected, and several murmured in agreement.

Grandfather motioned with his hand in frustration. "Your lives are more valuable than these things!"

Above the ensuing murmuring, Grandmother's voice rose. "Also, be open to accepting aid by whoever is a follower of Riaas. As thanks, offer them a word and bless them."

Paxton could see the strain his grandparents were under. It made him angry when others questioned them while they were only doing their best to protect the flock. He knew them both as priests as well as grandparents and growing up under their love and tutelage had only cemented his admiration more.

As the meeting ended and people began leaving, Grandfather approached. "Be strong, Paxton. Don't lose faith." Placing a hand on Paxton's shoulder, he fiercely whispered, "You will one day take my place as high priest to carry on our order for future generations. One day our people will return."

Wiping the back of his hand across his nose, Paxton sniffed and nodded. Was Grandfather sharing a word from Riaas? It sounded like it. He knew Grandfather meant well, but those weren't the words he wanted to hear. He had asked them both many times to reconsider their decision, even though they had already explained their reasons for staying and wouldn't budge on the matter. They believed it was their duty to stand by the word that Riaas had spoken, even if that meant death. They were convinced that, if everyone fled, the king would not only go after them but also after their loved ones as well as any other temple supporters. His grandparents wanted to avoid that outcome. A few could die for the sake of the many. Some of the older clergy also volunteered to stay back, insisting that they were too old to make the journey and they had already lived full lives with no regrets. There wasn't a dry eye in the room that day.

Those who were leaving loved ones behind were encouraged to write letters. Those who had volunteered to stay behind would send them, once everyone had made it across the border. It was safer to say their goodbyes that way.

It's what Paxton's roommate, Henry, was doing that afternoon when they both had a bit of free time. Paxton resented watching Henry write goodbye letters to loved ones who weren't in any danger. They usually got along well, so this brewing hostility toward his close friend took Paxton by surprise.

He might as well walk along the courtyard's peristyle instead of fuming in his room. It was square-shaped with twelve columns for each colonnade. Hopefully, he wouldn't see anyone who wanted to engage him in conversation. It was common for others to ask him about the latest happenings or how he was doing, and these past weeks had become almost unbearable, as someone always seemed ready to corner him. Even though Paxton was adept at making excuses for why he wasn't available to stop and chat, he was relieved to see that today the colonnades mostly were clear of people.

Exercise and fresh air were what he needed until he noticed the new novice with the unusual ash-colored hair between the widely-spaced columns. The girl was playing with several young children in the green open space of the garden courtyard, children who belonged to some of the ordained couples. Hearing her easy laughter rankled him. How could she carry on like there was nothing bad happening? His anger spiked so much that he turned sharply and went back inside through the closest available door.

A GOOD PORTION OF PAXTON'S last days at the temple were spent helping to move and organize things. All of the scrolls with documented past words needed specially sealed containers and books needed storing. He didn't realize they had so many books on a wide range of topics. The books and scrolls were carefully placed in the underground vault inside the temple, along with heavier items like ornate furniture, marble statues, and gilt-framed paintings.

Everyone leaving Livania – the ordained, the younger and older novices, the guards, other staff, and immediate family members – wore traveler's clothes. Everyone who owned temple and monastery robes and slippers packed them for the journey. If anyone asked where they were going, they answered that they were making a pilgrimage to the temple of Riaas in Penthia.

Whether he was working or relaxing, Paxton tried to stay near his grandparents. Knowing he wouldn't be seeing them again, he wanted to be a comfort to them, but if he were honest, it was him who needed the comfort more. He watched how they set their worries aside and continued caring for the flock, including the visitors. Those seeking shelter would get upset when they were turned away, being told the temple was closing for a time. For a time? Paxton knew better. It would be a lot longer than that. Even the Karpydosan pilgrims were advised not to tarry in Livania. And Paxton would fume whenever the people didn't understand it was for their own good.

Chapter 6
Bitter Betrayal

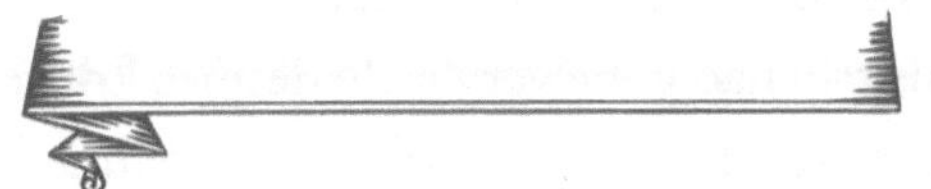

LORD GERAINT OF ELMSBRIDGE whistled one tune after the other as he and the prince rode side-by-side through the Kingdom of Karpydosa on their way back home to Livania. It was working out for the best that his favorite blue-roan stallion had had to stay behind. The morning of their departure to Karpydosa, Dusk had been a little off in his right foreleg. Geraint hoped it hadn't been anything serious and looked forward to seeing him again. His next choice had been Cobble, his chunky bay gelding. Cobble was the most comfortable horse to ride, having very smooth gaits and, being gelded, didn't cause a ruction with any of the mares. Yes, for such a long journey, Cobble was turning out to be the better choice.

It was a beautiful day, and since Prince Edson was deep in thought, Geraint amused himself with whistling. He was pleased with how well things had gone at Strondor Castle in Karpydosa. They were deemed important enough that the prince's entourage was being escorted to the Bay of Brothers by thirty of King Marin's soldiers, where a ship would be awaiting them. The king had insisted on strengthening the number of Prince Edson's fighting men, something about bandits recently causing trouble. The Karpydosan soldiers were taking them along a different route, avoiding the area where the bandits were most active. Ten of Marin's men led the way, and twenty brought up the rear.

Besides Edson and Geraint, the entourage from Livania consisted of two merchants and two nobles, five grooms, eight servants, the cook, ten of Edson's personal guards, and twenty of his father's best-trained men. They had left Livania in a hurry and kept their group small so that they could travel quickly. It took their delegation two weeks, pushing hard, to get from the castle to the bay and then another two days to get to Strondor Castle. They didn't want to risk delays when Prince Jurem's life was hanging in the balance.

Geraint looked at the four older men as he continued whistling. The merchants and nobles were closer in age to King Arlo and were part of his group of friends and advisors. The king had a vested interest in this small delegation and wanted to ensure a favorable outcome. Geraint figured things couldn't have gone any better and was certain they would be returning with a good report. Yes, this trip had gone very well, despite Edson's initial misgivings. Edson only made the trip because his father commanded it. Geraint still felt bad about that, and his whistling faltered. Their father-son relationship was not the warmest. Edson carried a heavy burden being the crown prince.

On a happier note, they had been given the best care as honored royal guests, and Geraint had relished it. Once the Crown Prince of Karpydosa was healed of his malady, they were treated like heroes. Jurem had been suffering from horrible symptoms, including chills, fever, vomiting, and mental confusion. It was so bad that Edson required a full day to heal him, only leaving the room to eat and rest. After giving so much of himself to Jurem's healing, Edson slept like the dead that night and needed another day to get his strength back.

The next day, Jurem was sitting in bed, weak, but free of the malady. Jurem had been washed and given all clean bedding. They had spent a good portion of the following days in his sitting room and small private garden talking about anything and everything while Jurem's strength returned.

Sharing the hero status with Edson was a perk of being close to the prince. Having people fawn over him did wonders for his ego. Geraint was the second son of a noble and a loyal friend and confidant to Edson. He was twenty-three, four years older than the prince. When the prince was five and he was nine, Geraint became Edson's playmate, but his main duty was to watch over the prince and keep him out of trouble. He knew Edson looked up to him, which he appreciated. But these past two years, Edson was becoming his own man, and Geraint understood that too.

Geraint looked over at the contemplative prince riding alongside. Edson was a handsome prince with high cheekbones and dark wavy hair like his father. He wore his hair in a ponytail to keep it out of his face, and his eyes were opalescent, typical of Livanians born with the healing gift. They contrasted nicely with his dark eyebrows and hair. An opal set in yellow and white gold hung on a thick chain around his neck, a symbol that he wore with pride.

They had spent almost two weeks with two lovely princesses, Jurem's younger sisters. Rose was eighteen and Lily sixteen. Both girls had made sweet eyes at the Livanian prince. Geraint had already set his heart on another princess, so it had amused him to watch these two try and capture Edson's attention, along with all the other eligible females they'd met at the castle. Edson had no obstacles preventing him from marrying a lady of his choosing, and Geraint envied him that.

They took their roles seriously, but Geraint preferred not to show it. Edson was serious enough for the both of them, so he made it his secondary mission to try and keep things light for the prince's sake. Geraint stopped his whistling and smiled. He rarely ever felt this happy and relaxed.

Cobble twitched his ears when the whistling stopped.

After moving his mount a bit closer, Geraint leaned over and gave Edson a friendly punch to the shoulder.

Edson turned with one eyebrow raised. "What was that for?"

"I was just thinking how everyone fawned over you. And, they couldn't seem to get enough of your eyes."

"Yes, well, no one with the gift of healing travels outside of Livania, as you know. I was the first," he said dryly.

"And, look how well it turned out! So much for worrying about the word your great-great-grandfather received."

Scowling, Edson replied, "Just because our visit went well doesn't mean that Livanian healers should take the risk and journey beyond our borders."

Geraint scratched his head. "Hmm. Well, you're probably right." He leaned sideways in the saddle and eyed the prince. "What I want to know is how you kept that bored expression on your face for most of the time. I mean, there were so many exquisite things to see, not to mention both of Jurem's younger sisters!"

"I did it intentionally. You know that my eyes flash if I feel any strong emotions." He loosened his hair tie and ran his fingers through his wavy hair. As he put his hair back into a ponytail, he said, "The Karpydosans were already gaping enough at me."

Geraint pulled a face. "I didn't realize it bothered you so much. Why didn't you say anything?"

The prince quirked an eyebrow and gave a half-smile. "I could see you were enjoying yourself, and I didn't want to spoil your fun."

"I'm supposed to protect you, not the other way around."

Edson waved Geraint's protest away. "Look, if it makes you feel any better, I was happy seeing you so happy." After taking a drink of water from his canteen, he added, "Listen, I would appreciate it if you don't go gushing to my father about how amazing everything was. It's already bad enough listening to him wishing we had what they have. It will only make it worse."

"Well, you better tell the rest of our party before they relay their accounts."

Edson took a glance behind him in the saddle. Geraint also turned to look back. The Karpydosan soldiers were trailing further behind as they entered a pass. Keeping his voice down, Edson said, "I plan to, once we're free of our extra escort."

When Geraint was certain the Karpydosan soldiers were far enough away, he put on his most cheeky smile and asked the question that Edson had been avoiding the past few days. "So, which flower do you prefer, Rose or Lily?"

Edson's expression turned sour. "You know, I don't think they would like to hear you referring to them in that way. They are princesses, don't forget."

Geraint tensed his hands and Cobble shook his head at the tightening of the reins. Not wanting to reveal how the prince's words affected him, he quickly loosened his grip. And that was the rub. They were princesses while he was just a lowly lord of a lesser house. Hiding his true feelings, he jokingly replied, "Their names are flowers, after all, so they can't complain." He sniffed and added, "But, my question still stands. Who do you prefer?"

A muscle in Edson's jaw ticked. "You know, if I say anything, I won't hear the end of it from you."

Geraint grinned. "So, you do like one of them? Which one?"

"Look, I thought Rose was nice. Okay? Now, let it rest."

Geraint slapped his thigh. "I knew it!"

Cobble snorted and shook his head.

The prince sighed in frustration. "You're one to talk. If anything, you should be grateful that I don't harass you about my sister."

"Oh, I don't know. I think I'd be happy if you did. I could talk about her all day long." He said the last three words in a sing-song voice.

At that, Edson made a face.

Geraint, having won that round, responded with a wide smile while giving Cobble a firm pat. The truth behind his jovial manner was much less happy. Whenever they were alone and Edson would mention Princess Anwen, he would make light of his interest in her. Geraint didn't want Edson, or anyone else for that matter, to know just how serious his feelings really were. He knew he didn't have much of a chance. He had nothing to offer, being a second-born noble and therefore not in line to inherit.

Considering all the time Geraint had spent with Edson's family, it was only natural that he had come to fall in love with Princess Anwen, regardless of their six-year age difference and his lack of station. She had her mother's beautiful blue eyes, but hers had a warmth and kindness to them that her mother's eyes lacked. Her hair was dark like her father's and brother's, and it cascaded below her shoulders, contrasting nicely against her porcelain skin.

It was impossible not to stare at her whenever she was nearby, so he'd become skilled at secretly watching her. She moved with grace and held her head high, yet she never flaunted her royal status. And when she went riding, Anwen sat her horse beautifully. She and her little grey mare seemed to meld into one graceful entity.

Not only was Anwen beautiful on the outside but also inside. She usually had a kind word, a ready smile, and a heart for those less fortunate. But if she felt uncomfortable or didn't like someone, she would turn formal and speak less.

Geraint sighed. These thoughts weren't helping him any. He had to keep reminding himself to accept the fact that one day she would marry a first-born noble or a foreign prince. He was neither.

Upon hearing an unusual bird call, Geraint sat straighter. He quickly glanced around. Something about that call didn't fit, and the path they were taking didn't feel right. "This doesn't look like a safe route."

The prince narrowed his eyes. "No, it doesn't."

They were being hemmed in by the narrowing of the pass and their escort had fallen back. The hairs on Geraint's neck prickled.

There were shouts and then the pounding of hooves as the Livanian guards in front began racing back. The horses stepped high and jostled their riders. Geraint looked back over his shoulder, and what he saw made his body turn to ice. The Karpydosan guards were forming a wall at their back, blocking any chance of retreat.

Geraint could finally make out the shouted words of his fellowmen over the pounding of the hooves. "It's a trap! To the prince!" Then he heard arrows fly and people scream.

As Geraint's mind caught up to the words, he whipped his head over to the prince. Edson's face had gone slack with shock. Geraint pushed off from his saddle and leaped, tackling Edson to the ground and away from the deadly rain of arrows. Trying to break the prince's fall with his own body got the wind knocked out of him. He stood as quickly as possible, coughing with tears streaming from his eyes. Edson was already on his feet and his sword drawn.

Livanian guards soon surrounded them, using their armored bodies and shields to protect them from arrows and stomping of hooves. Their horses' hooves were dangerous, but the size of their equine forms also provided some protection.

Edson's eyes flashed, and he snarled. "We've been betrayed."

Those were the last words Geraint heard from his prince as they began fighting for their lives.

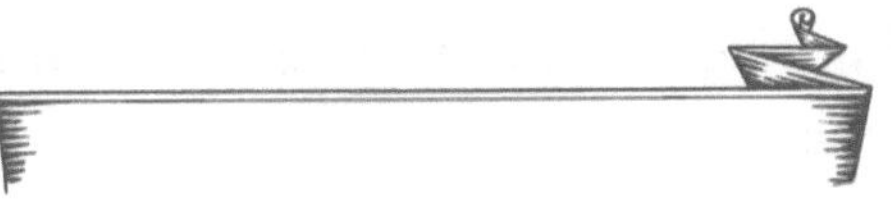

Chapter 7
Stolen Stone

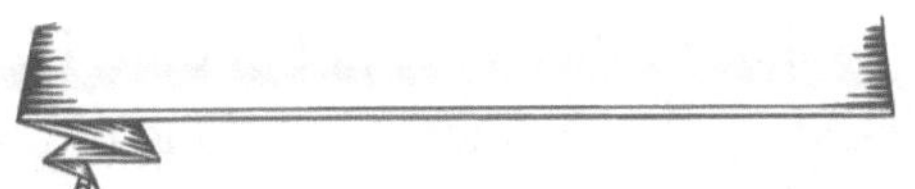

ONCE GERAINT CAME TO, the stench of blood, vomit, and voided bowels assaulted his senses. There was a pounding in his head and a great weight upon his chest. He was dizzy, sick, and bewildered. Even slight movements threatened his tenuous grip on consciousness. Then he heard voices, and something inside him told him to remain still. As the voices drew near, he tried focusing on their words through the pain and dizziness. They were speaking in Emirlinn, the common tongue.

While lying still, Geraint felt the weight on his chest momentarily lessen and then return with a thud. It was the hardest thing not to grimace or cough.

"Hey, we were promised the spoils!" said a gruff impatient voice with an accent he didn't recognize.

"Except for the opal. That wasn't included." The man closest to Geraint replied with a distinct Karpydosan accent.

Alarmed, Geraint steeled himself not to flinch. *Oh, no! Edson was wearing his opal on a gold chain when we were attacked!*

"Yes. That was the deal," said a third and more nondescript voice. Something confident in the oily tone made Geraint think he must be the leader.

"What do they want with it?" asked the first speaker. "It's pretty, but what makes this one so special? Seems like a lot of trouble for a hunk of multicolored rock."

"Don't worry about the opal. We have enough here to keep us busy for a while. And be quick about it. We've got to make it across to Bariny before nightfall."

Rough hands grabbed Geraint, and the weight on his chest was lifted once more. He remembered just in time to remain limp and let his face go completely slack. When he was pulled into a sitting position, his head rolled forward and over to the side. The sudden motion was too much for him, and he blacked out for the second time that day.

AS GERAINT SLID TOWARD waking, he almost moaned. Remembering he was in danger, he swallowed the sound just in time. He held his breath and listened. His ears picked up the distinctive croaking of ravens and the lighter cawing of carrion crows further away, but no human voices or sounds of horses. An overwhelming battlefield stench blew into his face, choking him and nearly making him gag. A buzzing of flies was incessantly loud. When a few landed on his face, the tickling was almost unbearable, but he stayed completely still, unsure if it was safe to open his eyes.

Gathering his courage, Geraint carefully cracked an eye open. As soon as he was sure there was no other movement, he slowly pushed himself upright. He blinked and swiped at his face with his sleeve to clear the stars and shadows swirling before his eyes.

Trying to make sense of the carnage all around him, he blinked again. Once his vision cleared, he narrowed his focus at the weight lying across his lower legs. It was Edson. But not his laughing friend. It was a bloodless parody with wide empty eyes staring sightlessly into space. Geraint reached forward unbelievingly, running his fingers over the huge slashes and rents in his friend's crimson-soaked clothing and the flesh underneath. He drew back his hand, feeling as though it didn't belong to him, as though he wasn't really even present.

Geraint gulped in a breath of fouled air and suddenly felt his stomach rebel. He leaned over onto his right side and threw up until nothing was left but bile. When it finally stopped, Geraint wiped his mouth on his right sleeve, pulled his legs from beneath Edson's body, and staggered to his feet.

As he looked around, he realized he hadn't been unconscious for long, which meant their attackers couldn't be far. The bodies he could see were very fresh, their congealing blood still wet and shiny and all completely stripped of valuables. Some even had ring-bearing fingers hacked off or ears cut for the small gold or silver hoops they'd been wearing. None had been allowed any dignity, as many even had their clothes cut away, leaving them exposed to any merciless scavengers.

Edson's gold chain with the opal stone was gone too. Geraint was glad he didn't wear jewelry often because, if he had... Well, he wouldn't have been able to hide that he was still alive, and they would have finished him off for sure. At least the mercenaries had been in a hurry and had missed the small sharp knife in Geraint's boot and the leather coin pouch tucked tightly against his body under his shirt and belt.

The moment Geraint took a step forward, his legs gave way. He sank to one knee and realized he was crying, tears sliding from his eyes and running down his face. He wiped absently at his face and nose with his sleeve. How could this be happening, everyone dead? His prince, dead. He was living a nightmare. Why wasn't he dead along with them?

Feeling sick and dizzy, Geraint struggled back to his feet, fighting to keep his balance. He steadied a little and felt himself over. On the side of his head was a huge lump. The wound must've bled profusely, judging from the crusty mass in his hair and down his neck. He must've taken quite a blow. He hoped they hadn't cracked his skull. He seemed to have escaped any other serious wounds barring a long shallow gash down his left arm. Most of the blood soaking his shirt and trousers didn't seem to be his. But whose was it?

His heart clutched tightly, and he groaned as he realized the awful truth. It was Edson's blood. Not only was Edson his prince and future king but also his best friend and as close as a beloved brother could be. These past fourteen years, from the time they were small boys, they'd been inseparable, studying, training, and getting into mischief together. Geraint had been Edson's sworn companion and was also supposed to be his last defense against any attacker!

He gulped and shuddered. He had failed him! The evidence of his failure was lying at his feet. As he looked down at his prince again, no, at his friend, those once brilliant eyes stood open and staring. Choked by grief and fresh tears streaming down his face, Geraint stooped over his best friend. Gently, he closed the lids over the eyes that would never dazzle anyone again, and then he sank, once again, onto his knees.

An unbearable thirst finally brought him back to his senses. Geraint wiped his face on a portion of his sleeve that wasn't bloodied. He allowed his gaze to sweep over the carnage. Geraint was convinced that none of the Livanians were meant to survive. Being alive was probably a serious mistake and one that they might want to rectify. He'd better get going.

While he quickly searched the ground, he found a canteen with a broken strap lying in the grass. Geraint didn't want to know who it belonged to, so he tried to avoid looking. He bent and picked it up, drank, and croaked out a quiet "thank you."

Well, since he wasn't dead, perhaps there were more survivors like him. The only way to find out was to go and check each body. It was a grim undertaking. Geraint screamed his grief at the ravens to get them to move out of his way while he searched. Muttering curses under his breath, he turned and examined one dead Livanian face after another. He knew them all, some from before and others he'd come to know on this journey. He'd played dice, traded stories, made jokes, and eaten with them. The brutality of their deaths and the stench made him throw up again. He no longer bothered wiping the tears.

How many Karpydosan soldiers had died? Geraint couldn't find any of them lying around. He hoped they had suffered; he needed them to have suffered. After rolling over the last body, he sat on a fallen log to rest, trying to make sense of everything. He drank more water from the canteen and wet a relatively clean cloth to wipe some of the blood and tears from his face and hands.

Geraint knew the Karpydosans were behind this attack by supposed bandits. They were clearly organized and efficient, trained fighting men, probably mercenaries hired for the job. Ordinary bandits were never so disciplined and seldom attacked armed parties of travelers. They didn't like taking risks. Geraint had been prepared to question any that he might find wounded, but there were none. He only found four of their dead compared to forty-nine Livanians. They had had the advantage of surprise and position. It was a well-planned and well-executed massacre of their delegation and a waste of good people's lives.

But why? Was this ambush all about Prince Edson's opal? It was a quality stone, but he'd seen far more valuable jewels while visiting Strondor Castle. It certainly wasn't worth murdering fifty people over. You'd have to be crazy to do something like that! Even though it didn't make any sense, it was the only conclusion Geraint could make.

Wounded and without a horse, Geraint was in a difficult situation. Poor Cobble. He was such a good horse, and Geraint would miss him. Those evil bastards! If he could, he'd chase them down and make them pay.

But he couldn't dwell on that now. Right now, he needed to clear his mind and focus on getting back to Livania. The most direct route back was sailing across the Bay of Brothers, but it would be too risky as any Karpydosan soldier might recognize him. No one would be on the lookout for him since he was presumed dead, along with the rest of the Livanians, but it would be just his luck to be spotted. The way things stood, Geraint would have to travel the long way through Bariny and, from there, cross into Livania. It wouldn't be easy, and Geraint had never traveled the route before. He didn't relish the thought of what lay ahead.

As he assembled a few items salvaged from the field, another unwelcome thought struck him. Would anyone return to the scene and notice that a person among the slain was missing? After a few moments of consideration, he decided the risk was small. The ravens and carrion crows were already busy, and, by nightfall, large predators would be too. Soon, no one would be recognizable. Geraint wasn't wearing anything notable or brightly colored either, so he should be safe. The ground had been churned up enough from men's boots and horses' hooves that it wasn't too difficult to hide his tracks, even in his slightly dizzy state.

Taking his bearing from the sun's position, Geraint began heading north. He wanted to carry the prince's body home with him, but that would be impossible. He would focus on what he could do. He owed it to Edson. He needed to tell the king, no, *not* the king; he needed to tell Edson's *father* what had happened here.

It didn't require a well-trained scout to follow the tracks left behind by the mercenaries. They hadn't bothered to try to disguise their route and, between their own mounts and the extra horses, had churned up the ground so that a blind man could have seen their direction. Geraint would never catch them on foot but that wasn't his plan. The only reason he followed them was that they knew the quickest route into Bariny. He remembered hearing one of them say that that was where they were going.

Geraint had never considered himself a violent man until today. Now he wanted revenge.

As he plodded along the trail, his feelings see-sawed wildly between sick remembrances, a desire for vengeance, shame at failing to protect Edson, and exhaustion mixed with pain. He felt so sick from it all that he wished he could lie down, and that today was yesterday. He wished he had a band of fighting men to take revenge, and he wished he could kill the attackers one by one with his bare hands. He knew the king would certainly seek retribution after hearing Geraint's account of today's events, and he hoped to participate in meting it out.

The tracks crossed a small rocky stream where Geraint could drink, refill his canteen, and wash his wounds. It was especially difficult getting the blood out of his hair. The water was so bitter cold he couldn't bear to soak his head for very long. His scalp burned like fire and Geraint was afraid he'd start it bleeding again if he poked at the wound, so he finally opted to let the flow of the river do the work. He managed to get most of the crusted blood, dead leaves, and dirt out, making him feel much better. He also washed his clothes, figuring they could dry as he walked. Wet and somewhat cleaner was better than dry and crusted with blood. He was also a lot less likely to attract the unwanted attention of predators. He was in no condition to try and fight off anything larger than a small fox.

Geraint was relieved to find mouse ear bushes growing prolifically along the river. It was early for the berries but he found enough half-ripe ones, somewhere between the colors of bright pink and dark blue, to quiet the grumbling of his belly. The large round leaves had different uses, especially pulping them for wounds and rashes. He didn't have any means of making pulp in the proper way, so he popped the leaves into his mouth and chewed them a bit until they were mushy. Tearing a somewhat clean section from his shirt into thin strips, Geraint applied the poultice to the wound on his left arm, tying it on with the strips. He picked himself up and continued walking. He still had a long way to go and the hour was growing late. He would walk as long as he could, wanting his clothes to dry before lying down to sleep.

The Karpydosans would not get away with their betrayal. Not if Geraint could do anything about it. Focusing on getting the truth to the king would be enough to keep him going and from being overwhelmed with grief and despair. There was, of course, the chance that King Arlo would hear his story and, with a flick of his fingers, condemn Geraint to death. He had, after all, failed in his most important task, to protect the crown prince. King Arlo had been known to execute people for far, far less. Well, he could do nothing to change his fate. Geraint could only do what he must to ensure that the senseless murder of his companions, and especially of Edson, did not go unpunished.

Chapter 8
Letter of Lies

THE VERY LATEST SHIPBUILDING plans lay open upon a large wooden table in front of King Arlo. His noble advisors, several wealthy merchants, and two of his most experienced artificers were sitting and standing around the table to get a better look as they discussed various aspects of the design. This group had met several times to discuss this grand new ambition for Livania's future. As Arlo was not yet ready to announce his plans, they were meeting in the small private withdrawing room located off the great chamber of state. Not only was it only accessible through one door, but it also boasted an efficient fireplace and some very comfortable chairs.

Drumming his fingers against the arm of his heavy maplewood chair, King Arlo stared at the plans with unfocused eyes. It was hard to concentrate on this latest project when Edson was so late in getting back. Something was wrong.

Arlo refocused on the men before him. They were discussing the logistics of building a merchant fleet, something that had been consuming his thoughts for some time. Even though the king knew these men were reliable and intelligent, he sometimes thought they were inadequate for such a huge task.

Arlo and Marin were not much more than toddlers when they first met during a state wedding. As boys and as young men, the sons of royalty were encouraged to meet with one another should occasions require visits of state. They had been keenly competitive ever since. Arlo sometimes felt as if he were a little brother always running and trying to catch up to Marin.

It seemed like King Marin constantly had the upper hand. He was a little older, he had his fleet, he had a prettier, younger wife, finer horses, his son had been born first... it was always something. It was extremely frustrating. He hoped Edson would return soon with a good report of his healing Marin's son for him. Arlo smirked at the thought. Attaining personal and trade connections among the nobles and merchants that accompanied him would also be welcome and profitable. Gaining an alliance was almost within his grasp, and it would help Arlo tremendously in so many ways. The high priest and priestess had given the Word. It would happen. But where was his delegation? They were late, something was wrong.

There was a sudden sharp rap on the door. The two guards stationed outside the room, knowing the king was awaiting news about Edson, weren't required to await the king's response before opening the door. Wilton, his head steward, accompanied by his army commander, brusquely entered, their faces tight with worry. Arlo tensed, and the room grew silent.

"Pardon me, Your Majesty." The steward bowed. "This message arrived just now from Karpydosa. It came by special messenger."

Arlo breathed in shallowly as he waved Wilton forward. No one spoke a word while the king stared at the packet sealed with Marin's royal crest. Why was Army Commander Balcom here? The letter was unopened, but they must know something of its contents. Perhaps the messenger had said something to Wilton. Having his commander accompanying his steward didn't bode well. Glancing at both men, he asked, "Did the messenger say what this was about?"

The commander spoke, "Yes, Your Majesty. We think you should read the letter first. Perhaps it will shed more light on the events the messenger described."

Grunting, Arlo broke the seal and slid the papers from the packet. Pulling them apart, he dropped a small map on the table and concentrated on the neatly written words. As he read, his face went white before turning red and his hands tightened on the thick cream-colored paper. While he held his breath for several heartbeats, the tension in the room could be felt.

The letter fell from the king's hands, fluttering onto the table's surface. The noble closest to him snatched it up. As he began reading aloud, the expressions of puzzlement and worry on the faces of everyone in the room turned to shock, horror, and disbelief.

Written this day by my own hand at Strondor castle,

To my friend, Arlo, King of Livania.

It is with a heavy heart and great regret I must write you today. I have only just received a message bearing news of such treachery that I can hardly bring myself to write of it to you. But I must as it concerns your son, Prince Edson.

My escort was very late returning from its duty to accompany your son and his entourage to their ship, causing my commander to send a search party to discover their whereabouts. We were horrified when a messenger arrived bearing a terrible tale of ambush, robbery, and murder. I am devastated to have to tell you that the entire Livanian delegation, including your son Edson with his constant companion Geraint, were all slaughtered by bandits as they travelled through the forest on their way to the bay. We discovered their horses and personal belongings stolen and no survivors.

I have sent men to track and apprehend these bandits, but we fear that they may have already escaped across the border into Bariny. Should that prove to be the case, I shall immediately send an urgent message to Tarson, King of Bariny, to request permission to hunt these filthy dogs on his land, and for his assistance to do it.

We have buried your people, and I have ordered prayers said and sacred fires lit for the repose of their souls in the afterlife. The one exception is your son, Prince Edson. His body has been prepared and sealed in a casket and will be transported home to you, for burial with his family. I ask that the men accompanying him on his final journey be provisioned and sent home as soon as they may.

Your son was a fine young man and showed great promise as a ruler. He successfully healed my own son of his mysterious malady and will forever have my gratitude, and be considered a friend and a savior of my house.

I will close this letter now, and send it with a special messenger to reach you as soon as possible. Know that I grieve with you and continue to hold out the hand of friendship as a bridge between our people.

THE NOVICE

With sadness,

Your friend, Marin, King of Karpydosa

The king rose from his chair. Shock, rage, and grief played over his face. "Where is the Karpydosan messenger who brought this? I will question him, and I *will* have answers. Then I will send him back to *his* king in ragged little pieces!"

"Sire, I believe you want your son's body returned to you. Killing this messenger would hinder that," said Balcom, his face and voice resolute.

"He arrived under the flag of a herald!" interjected Wilton. "He is only a messenger, and, as an official herald bearing a message, he is guaranteed immunity from any kind of retribution!"

Arlo narrowed his eyes at Wilton. The man was shaking with fear. Well, he should be. Arlo wasn't a man to cross. "Then get me every one of those lying priests at the temple!"

The king pointed at Commander Balcom with his arm outstretched. "I want them all. Every damned one of them. The ordained, the novices, old, young, all of them. I want every person in that thrice-damned temple dragged here in chains and imprisoned in the cells." He pointed straight down. Then his voice took on a terrifying snarling quality. "I will decide their fate and there won't be enough words in the world from their false god to save them."

Chapter 9
Powerful People

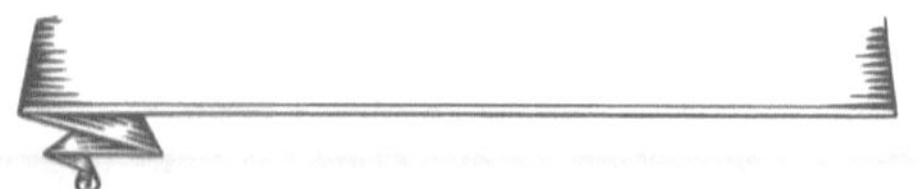

IT TOOK GERAINT TWO days to walk into Bariny, but once he did, he stopped following the tracks left behind by the mercenaries. Their path continued in a northerly direction, but he needed to head northwest toward the Amesvar River, the natural border between Bariny and Livania.

He bought bread, cheese, and a small flask of watered wine from a short skinny peddler he met on the road, a peddler who seemed very skittish about the transaction and who seemed only too glad to be on his way. Self-preservation was inbred in the peddler folk, and he acted like he could smell trouble wafting off Geraint. And, Geraint mused to himself, the little man wasn't wrong.

After four days on foot, Geraint came upon a friendly young farmer and his wife and four children. They were working in a small cabbage field beside their little stone house surrounded by a fence. His food was long gone, and he was famished. His lips were chapped, his feet blistered, and he was suffering from fever from an infected arm, constant headaches, and a sense of deep depression.

Calling out to the farmer, he asked if an inn was nearby. Upon hearing that the nearest village was further on, about an hour's walk, he wavered and leaned heavily against the fence. The farmer walked rapidly over to him. Taking his arm, he helped him to a wooden bench in the shaded dooryard. He directed the oldest of the four children to fetch some water from the well while his wife shooed the younger children away.

Once they made their brief introductions, Farmer Tom asked Geraint if bandits had attacked him. As Geraint opened his mouth to answer, Tom turned and, rather dramatically, told his wife that he had been. And Joan, Tom's wife, seemed to go along with his interpretation of Geraint's disarray. Taken aback,

Geraint closed his mouth without making any corrections. It was certainly easier than having to explain everything he'd been through in the last week.

The couple agreed to allow Geraint to stay for a few days. They gave him the children's large bed under the narrow extended roof on one side of the house. If he positioned himself sideways, it would accommodate his long frame. They also fed him very well. He had never eaten pork stewed with apples before and resolved to ask Cook about it when he got back. The happy atmosphere with the children being excited about sleeping in the loft with blankets covering the hay was almost enough to stop his nightmares.

Geraint stayed until his fever broke, which took only two days, under the expert care of the children's mother. She cautioned him against overuse of his arm and gave him a small pot of a sharp-smelling salve to apply to his rapidly healing wounds.

After bargaining a bit, they sold him everything he needed, including a sturdy black pony to continue his journey, fresh clothing, a blanket, and a few other camping essentials. Joan packed his provisions, and Tom helped him to settle the saddlebags properly behind the saddle on the pony's broad back. Geraint was grateful for their help, paid the agreed-upon amount, and then handed Joan his last silver coin. He told her to buy something special for the children at Midsummer, then mounted up and prepared to go.

Tom thanked him and said. "By the way, the pony's called Blackie, and he knows the name."

Geraint nodded and smiled. Turning the pony, he headed up the road. He made good time. Blackie wasn't fast, but he never seemed to tire. Geraint made only one stop by a stream where he and Blackie could drink and rest for a few hours in the darkest part of the night.

When he arrived at the border the following afternoon, the captain on duty on Livania's side recognized him. The captain couldn't leave his post, but he could spare a few men to escort him along with horses. They would be swapping their horses out for fresh ones to shorten the time, but it would still be another week of hard riding. A messenger, who would be traveling at a much faster pace riding specially bred and highly conditioned messenger horses, rode on ahead to notify the king of their imminent arrival.

The captain assured Geraint that Blackie would be cared for. Geraint would miss the pony's steady companionship and the bit of freedom he'd experienced on the road. Now his future was in the hands of others. If the king allowed him to live, he'd send someone to bring Blackie to the castle and royal stables. And if he would ever be able to marry and have kids, then Blackie would be the one to teach them how to ride. But something like marriage and children didn't seem possible when Geraint's heart was for the princess. And depending on how things turned out, he might not even have a future.

Geraint couldn't decide if he wanted to be at the castle as quickly as possible and get it over with or never get there.

As they traveled, the escort told Geraint what the letter from King Marin had said about the ambush and death of Prince Edson and his delegation. Even though Geraint had been anticipating some form of lie, hearing of King Marin's letter with its sympathy and declarations of friendship made him sick. Geraint became so enraged at Marin's duplicity that his emotions leaked out. His horse repeatedly tossed his head and snorted as they trotted steadily up the road.

At least Geraint could tell these men the real story about that day. But then they said something else shocking. King Arlo had been enraged at the prince's death and the failed prophecy. He then had everyone at the Temple of Riaas arrested and dragged in chains to the city square where their crime against the crown was announced to the good citizens of Tilmar. Afterwards, they were carted off and thrown into the cells below the castle. Even more shocking was that most of the Servants of Riaas were no longer in the kingdom. They were gone, fled to Penthia. King Arlo flew into a fury and swore that he would have his vengeance. He hadn't yet made his next move, but for now, he was happy to leave the high priest and priestess, along with the other dozen of ordained, languishing below the castle. He would still make an example of them, that was certain.

Geraint shared in the king's desire for revenge, except that his anger was at King Marin and his betrayal. Even as he sought revenge for Edson's death, a small voice questioned if the Servants of Riaas were at fault. They were the ones who had told the king that Livania and Karpydosa would one day form a strong alliance. If they hadn't said so, none of this would have happened! So many questions swimming through his head made his headache worse.

As Geraint began to sway in the saddle, his escort called a stop, taking the opportunity to eat and rest the horses. Once Geraint felt strong enough, he told the men what really happened the day that the delegation was attacked.

Relaying the events stirred Geraint up all over again. The need for revenge was pumping through his blood, strong enough to drown out any worries he might have had for the Servants of Riaas.

They finally arrived after a week of hard riding. It was late afternoon, and the captain of the king's guard was waiting for them inside the castle courtyard. Captain Arten was in his early forties with wavy brown hair and a trim mustache and beard. He was all solid muscle of medium build, the kind of man you wouldn't mess with, but he was also fair. He greeted Geraint in a reserved manner, causing Geraint's stomach to tighten with apprehension. At least the captain was an open-minded man, something Geraint appreciated, especially when he didn't yet know what his reception would be once he saw the king.

After the very brief greeting, two of the captain's men escorted Geraint to a bathing chamber where servants were waiting to help him wash. They had kept an eye out for his arrival, as the fast messenger had arrived the previous day. All had been made ready, so there was no time to go to his rooms. Geraint was relieved to be completely clean again, his beard trimmed short and wearing clothes that fit. Arten and the two men then escorted Geraint to the withdrawing chamber where, he heard, the king, along with his advisors, was impatiently awaiting him.

One of two guards standing outside the chamber opened the door a crack and stood back to allow them through. Stepping brusquely toward the partially opened door, Geraint overheard one of the nobles speaking about the princess. He froze in his tracks at the words he heard, the captain nearly crashing into him. "We must discuss suitable husbands for Princess Anwen now that she is next in line to the throne." It felt like a stone had dropped inside his stomach. Geraint would never be on the list of suitable husbands.

"Yes, I have been considering this already. As soon as I select someone, the marriage will take place. I want someone who is unquestionably loyal to me and who will not hesitate to do what's necessary." The king's voice was so unlike him, cold and devoid of inflection, and it chilled Geraint.

Arten gave Geraint a sideways look and pushed past him. Entering the room with the door now wide open, he bowed. "Your Majesty, Geraint is here."

Geraint was still trying to collect his thoughts when all eyes fastened on him. The room had gone silent at Captain Arten's announcement, but soon there was a buzz of murmuring as Geraint hastily followed him in. The room was uncomfortably warm from the fire in the hearth and people filling the space. Merchants, nobles, and officers, including Commander Balcom, were seated while guards stood against the walls. Several of those seated also held glasses of wine. He wondered how long they had been waiting. They made room for Geraint and the captain and his men. It helped that the impressive table typically occupying the center of the room was notably absent.

King Arlo was seated on a throne-like chair. Though his sleeves were pushed up above his elbows, his posture was far from relaxed. His expression was tight, his grey eyes were like ice, and his forearms were corded.

"Your Majesty," Geraint said with a formal bow, unease prickling his neck. The atmosphere in the room was tense. He recognized the men seated, but what put him even more on edge were those who weren't in attendance, for instance, his father and brother. This meeting, then, was not intended to be a welcoming one.

Ironically, the king began by saying, "Lord Geraint, welcome." But he said it in a way that lacked all warmth. "We had thought you dead, and now we have the pleasure to see that this is not so." The king seemed far from pleased, and Geraint tried not to tremble. "However, I am troubled that you are alive, but the same cannot be said of my son." An air of threat laced the king's words, and the lack of inflection was terrifying.

Geraint nodded, taking a moment to steady his voice. "I completely agree, sire. There have been many times that I wished that I had died and the crown prince had lived." He paused, swallowing a painful lump in his throat. "Those who killed your son believed me to be dead with all the others. None of us were meant to survive that day. The only thing that has kept me alive when I wanted to give up, was the knowledge that I owed my king the truthful tale of what happened to his son, and to the others who fell beside him." What Geraint really thought, but didn't say, was that he owed it to Edson more than anyone else.

The king frowned, pursed his lips, and sat back in his chair. "So, tell us. What really happened that day? We were told that your party was ambushed by bandits. What none of us can understand is how any group of unorganized bandits could overpower a unit of Livanian fighting men and leave none of them alive. With the exception of yourself, of course." The unspoken question hung in the room that had gone suddenly silent.

Geraint's throat seized up, making it impossible to swallow past the dry lump. A sympathetic noble handed him a glass of wine. Geraint took a few inelegant gulps and then let out a breath. "Sire, you are correct. Mere bandits would not have succeeded, but these men were not bandits. They were trained men. Mercenaries. And they had help. A unit of thirty Karpydosan soldiers was with us as an escort. We were told they were there for our safety, but they were actually there to assist the mercenaries and take us by surprise. When the mercenaries attacked us, the Karpydosans joined them."

King Arlo sat forward, eyes glittering dangerously. "Do you have proof?"

Geraint began a full accounting of what happened that day and his ordeal to get word to the king. Someone offered him a seat, which he accepted gratefully and continued to speak. At the start of his tale, the feeling in the room was one of shock but soon became more and more outraged. Quietly muttered curses turned to loud exclamations the longer he spoke. The king and his army commander asked him to repeat parts of his story while someone else took notes. Once they were satisfied with his answers, they allowed others in the room to ask their questions.

One of the nobles asked, "Why do you think they wanted Prince Edson's opal? It was not an especially valuable gem, nor did it hold any special significance in and of itself. It wasn't even very old."

"Your Majesty, may I?" Dur, the wealthiest and oldest merchant present, rose and faced the king. Once a fierce caravan guard turned formidable merchant, he was tall and broad as a blacksmith. Despite his age, he was still handsome, his thick silver hair braided down his back in an unfashionable tail. One of his big scarred hands gripped a heavy oak cane topped with a solid silver wolf head, his only concession to the passage of time. Geraint hoped he'd look as good as him forty years from now.

Arlo nodded and Dur continued, commanding the room as he began to impart knowledge in his customary teaching voice, "Rumors are circulating in merchant circles of magical gemstones being mined in Yalamar and Salova. Some of these are said to generate heat or cold. The most common ones are supposed to give off light. The rarer ones are less known, and their abilities are held secret. It is thought that some may prolong a person's life for decades or can heal serious illnesses or defects of the mind or body."

"I thought those were only travelers' tales," said the king, waving his hand dismissively. "Like the tales of flying dragons or magic potions that make you invisible."

"Rumors often have some element of truth behind them," Dur spoke confidently, his deep voice rumbling. He nodded slowly, and when Arlo glared at him, he didn't even flinch. He had been part of various royal advisory councils for decades and was well acquainted with the snits and sulks of royalty. Geraint was impressed by the older man's demeanor. He wasn't sure that Dur's attitude towards Arlo was wise, but it filled him with admiration all the same.

"If this were so, then why aren't we seeing these magical stones, where our foreign trade is flourishing?" asked the noble who had spoken first.

"Both nations have an agreement in the movement of these gems," replied Dur. "The kings are brothers by marriage, and they are keeping tight control over them. Purchasing such a gem is not simple, as proper permits are required. Receiving a permit for one of the rarer ones is nearly impossible, and no miner or merchant would dare risk imprisonment or death for selling to someone without the proper permission. The gems don't come cheaply either. The entire treasury of Livania would barely pay for one such jewel of the rarer kinds."

King Arlo stared at Dur, and asked slowly, "So, do you think Marin believed Edson had a magical gem, perhaps a healing stone?"

"Yes, that is my guess, sire."

People began to murmur at this new development. Magic stones? The concept seemed unbelievable.

The king silenced everyone with his hand. Narrowing his cold eyes at his advisors, he said, "I am sure Marin has figured out by now that he was sorely mistaken about the opal. I find some small consolation in this. However, he cannot get away with murdering my son! He will pay for his actions." The king looked at Balcom. "Commander, prepare for war."

A muscle in the commander's jaw twitched, but he turned to the captain and spoke a few quiet words. Arten nodded and then left with both of his guards.

The commander was a big man, solid in every way, and affectionately known by the men as "Bull Mastiff" Balcom. But, at present, he was tugging on his sleeves and frowning. He was clearly unhappy and uncertain. "May I speak, sire?"

The king stared with eyes like hard cold stone. "What is it, Commander?"

"We must discuss how we plan to go about making King Marin pay for his duplicity."

King Arlo pinched the bridge of his nose. Pushing out a slow breath, he focused on the commander. "Go ahead, I'm listening."

Drumming his fingers against his thighs, Balcom took a moment before answering. "It will be impossible for us to get our army at full strength across the Bay of Brothers. We have very few ships. And even if we could get them across all at once, we would still be facing the Karpydosan army, which is superior in numbers and strength."

"Are you suggesting that we don't retaliate and that we allow them to get away with this atrocity? With murdering my son, your prince?!" The king's voice rose sharply, his words echoing like a slap.

Balcom rubbed the back of his neck. "No. What I am saying is that we must find another way to make them pay. Something where our smaller fighting force will not matter."

An uncomfortable silence followed.

Another merchant named Finis, whom Geraint was not at all fond of, ponderously took to his feet. "Your Majesty, we can take revenge on the Karpydosans who are in Livania. There are several hundred of their citizens here, merchants with their families doing business, some seeking healing, or even others on pilgrimage to the Temple of Riaas. That would certainly send a message to King Marin." Finis pulled a cloth from his pocket and dabbed at his round face. "We can confiscate their goods and property and arrest and enslave them. We can sail our ships from the Bay of Brothers southward to the Kingdom of Elnore and make use of their slave markets." Spreading his arms out wide, Finis added, "As you can see, there are a number of opportunities to recoup gold here."

There was more murmuring, with some expressions of shock at the suggestions.

Finis rubbed his thick hands together and smiled a rather unpleasant little smile. "Not that mere gold could possibly make up for the loss of Prince Edson. However, I do have the names and holdings of the Karpydosan merchants in Livania. I can supply a list to aid in this revenge."

Another noble stood up, "What happens when King Marin sends his army here?"

The commander answered, "He will have the same trouble getting an army across the bay. We can also close our borders, guard them, and perhaps plow up the roads, making it even more difficult."

Geraint stood, his voice firm despite his exhaustion. "I want to take part in these plans. What happened to us in Karpydosa was despicable. Prince Edson was loyal and true to his king. As a friend to the Karpydosan royal house, he gave his best while doing his duty, and he died too young and by treachery." Geraint's voice hitched at the end.

Arlo nodded and rubbed a hand down his face, suddenly looking much older than his years. He looked at Geraint and gave another nod. "You may lead men in some part of this plan, but we must move quickly and decisively. News must not get out, or our quarry will flee. Go! Eat and rest while we make plans. We will need a few days to improve our defenses, to make it difficult for Marin to retaliate."

Chapter 10
Riaas' Refugees

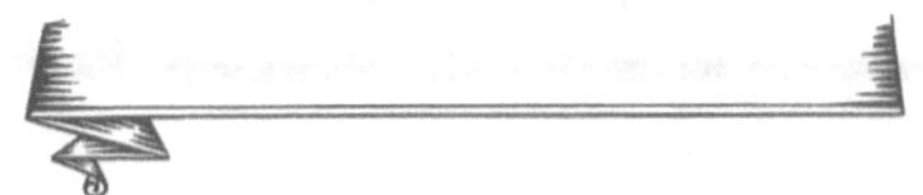

A LITTLE OVER A MONTH ago, Amity had had to leave her new home at the monastery and flee Livania. It was not what she had dreamed for her future. From what Amity understood, one man had upended her life, namely the king of Livania. Previously, she'd never thought much about the king as his world was so far apart from hers. And she'd always imagined the high priest and priestess were almost of equal standing. Now she knew better. The king had supreme power and did as he pleased.

Before she'd left the monastery, Amity had cared for ten young children between the ages of two and six. They belonged to some of the ordained. Their parents were making preparations for the journey. And this was how she'd ended up leaving along with the first group with the younger children and several adults, just under forty people. They had two horse-drawn wagons, two spare horses, and enough provisions to get them to Bariny.

They had journeyed southeastward for a little over two weeks until they reached the Amesvar River, bordering the Kingdom of Livania and the Kingdom of Bariny. Their group had traveled the most direct route through Livania to the closest toll bridge. As there were such young children with them crossing the border, to avoid suspicion, the adults said they were visiting a baron in Bariny, which was true. After paying the toll, they were on their way again, heading toward the baron's estate. It was another two days traveling in Bariny before they reached the manor house.

The kind baron had been expecting them, having been notified of their arrival ahead of time. He and his family were devout followers of Riaas. He'd arranged for the motley group of refugees to stay at his manor house and the surrounding buildings. Amity had cried tears of relief that first night because of their kindness and hospitality.

When Amity was making her way to Bariny, she'd felt the weight of guilt, leaving in secret, like a thief, without saying a proper goodbye to her family. They should have received her letter by now. She wondered how they felt about it. Would they be angry with her? Would they cry? Some of the younger novices like herself had chosen to go home. Amity could have done that too, but her dream was to serve Riaas. It didn't matter if she did that in Livania or Penthia.

In the two weeks she'd been in Bariny, other groups arrived almost daily. Some groups traveled the same route as theirs, but others journeyed over a different toll bridge not to attract too much notice. Several adults used that time to procure provisions for the journey ahead. They had to buy more of everything for the entire group, including horses and wagons to carry it all. In the meantime, the novices were busy with assigned chores.

Amity hadn't had a chance to make friends with the other girls. When together, they barely included her in their conversations. She was from a small town, and they were city girls. Actually, one of the girls grew up close to a city. That girl put in a lot of effort trying to be like them, but Amity was happy being herself.

Surprisingly, when the novices were assigned chores, Sereen and Laree had volunteered to help watch the little ones. They were just a year older, and Amity had high hopes of finally making friends. But she soon discovered that her "helpers" were only interested in talking to each other while ignoring Amity and the children. When the little ones requested they join in the games, the girls declined.

Amity saw how disappointed the children were, so she asked Sereen and Laree nicely if they would please participate, but she only received haughty expressions in return. What could she do? Nothing. She would make enemies if she told on them, so she kept quiet. After the third day, those two girls ended up on dish duty. The children had spoken up, but Amity was the one who got blamed. She wondered if things would go from bad to worse, and, of course, they did.

Paxton and his parents arrived at the end of the second week in the last group. They had a day to rest before the entire group of refugees continued their journey east toward the Whistling Mountains with the new provisions, horses, and wagons. The total number of clergy, staff, and children reached about four hundred. Most of the journey would be on foot, although anyone could rest in the wagons if needed.

The few times Amity glimpsed Paxton, he looked sullen and angry. It was too bad about his grandparents. Amity had overheard some of the ordained talking about the situation and sharing their fears. Paxton had a right to be upset, but he still had his parents and friends when Amity had no one, so what he did to her a few days later was inexcusable.

Ever since the incident with Sereen and Laree getting punished with dish duty, Amity got branded a snitch. Now her peers gave her the cold shoulder or made snide comments. None of what they were saying was true, of course, but Amity didn't really have anyone to take her side.

For some reason, Paxton began targeting her too. Adding insult to injury, he began calling her Ashes, because of her ash-brown hair, and the name stuck. Soon everyone, Paxton's age and younger, was calling her Ashes, including the little ones.

At least the children weren't mean about it. The best part about looking after them was that they kept her busy and away from the others with their nasty comments. They seemed to have boundless energy, talking happily as they walked. In Amity's opinion, they just wanted to hear themselves talk. And their questions were often silly too, but sometimes they got good discussions going.

Usually, the children were a lot of fun, but they were also a lot of work. After being on the road for several days, all that walking had quickly turned monotonous. They could only marvel at flocks of birds and patches of flowers so many times in the run of a day. As they grew too tired to walk, they could ride in the wagons, but those carried provisions for the journey. Sad little faces pulled at Amity's heart. Knowing that this journey would take many weeks, she tried making it as pleasant for them as possible.

The children didn't notice the slow passing of time when happily occupied. One of the things they did for fun was to sing songs. They sang old favorites, and Amity taught them a few new ones that she'd made up back home. One of those songs soon became a new favorite among the little ones. It started out slowly the first time around and sped up with each repeat until everyone tripped over their words and started laughing.

La la diddy doddy doh
How do sounds in nature go?
When horses go trot, you can hear clip-clop.
Clip-clop, clip-clop
Rain may go splatter or pitter-patter.
Splish-splash, splish-splash
The breeze can rustle the leaves of the trees.
Swish-swoosh, swish-swoosh
Bees buzz, collecting pollen with their fuzz.
Buzz-buzz, buzz-buzz
When the eagle flies, you will hear its cries.
Ee-ee, ee-ee
A donkey will bray when it's time for hay
Hee-haw, hee-haw
A piggy will squeal awaiting its meal.
Oink-oink, oink-oink
And a frog can croak by using his throat.
Ribbit, ribbit
La la diddy doddy doh
How do sounds in nature go?

Everyone fell into a routine. At night, just before exhaustion would pull her down into a deep sleep, Amity would wonder what her parents and sisters were doing. How were the wedding plans coming along? Would her big sister, Esme, think of Amity on her joyous day? Tears would fall from Amity's eyes as she thought about home. She held her gifts from Mama and Papa each night for comfort, placing them near her pillow.

What about Amity's future once they reached the distant land of Penthia? Would they be welcomed at the temple? It was difficult not to give in to worry or fear.

And what about the ordained who had volunteered to stay behind to face the king's wrath? She would shiver, thinking about their fate. Was it Fate, or was it Destiny? Priest Jerome had given lessons on the difference between Fate and Destiny back at the monastery, but she still wasn't sure. Sleep would soon steal her thoughts, and the next day would start all over again.

Then, one day, her hand glass from Mama and her little brocade purse with silver coins from Papa went missing. Princess Fee Fee and two other girls she shared the tent with insisted they knew nothing, but Amity suspected them. Those were her two most precious things from home and irreplaceable. She'd felt lonely before, but now she felt robbed of everyone and everything.

Chapter 11
Determined Damsel

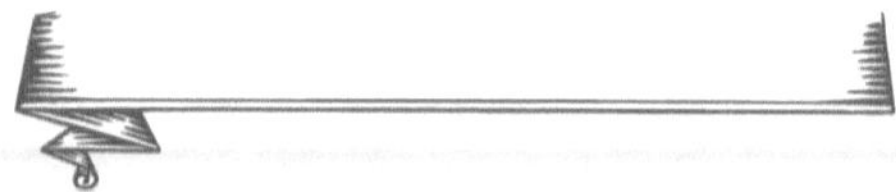

PRINCESS ANWEN SAT impatiently beside Mother in the great chamber, awaiting news regarding the latest commotion. The room was large and rectangular with golden-stained oak flooring and large square leaded-glass windows along one side overlooking the courtyard below. Box-shaped wooden chairs with low straight backs and armrests at right angles lined the opposite wall with colorful hanging tapestries depicting figures of Livanian history behind them. When the room was in use for balls, celebrations, or royal business, there was often a fire in the large stone fireplace, and the hanging candelabra and wall sconces would burn brightly. But the two women were here alone, so no cheery fires were burning, only two side lamps.

After Anwen had caught wind of some urgent meeting in the withdrawing chamber, having overheard two guards speaking quietly around the corner from her rooms, she'd quickly gone to fetch Mother. Despite Mother questioning her maid, they still didn't know any details of what had happened. That didn't stop them from wanting to hear the news firsthand or as close to that as possible.

It had seemed as though they were the last to find out about everything, including the horrifying news about Edson's death. When King Marin's letter had come, there had been an increased amount of whispering and tiptoeing going on at the castle before Father had finally come to tell them. They shouldn't have had to rely on overheard conversations and servants' gossip. She and Mother had had a right to know sooner! But Father believed that women belonged in the solar, perhaps in the kitchen or stillrooms, certainly in their bedchambers, and occasionally out walking the trails on a "suitable" pony, but definitely not around his advisors and where significant affairs of State took place.

Both women wore long black veils over their hair and black dresses. It was Livanian tradition to remain in black or very dark grey for six months for the passing of a close relative, an entire year if it was a spouse, and after that, dull colors for another six months or so, but without the veil. Mother was seated on her smaller throne beside Father's larger one under the red and black canopy at one end of the room. There was a door to one side of the thrones, leading to the private withdrawing chamber. Anwen sat beside her mother on a slightly lower throne-like chair while Edson's was on the opposite end, beside Father's. Her chest grew tight, and tears leaked from her eyes. Edson would never again sit in his rightful place. His empty chair was yet another reminder of the hole he had left behind in her heart.

Why did Edson have to die so young? She missed him so! He had been a wonderful brother and had allowed her to join in games with him and his companions. He'd read to her when she was little and had healed even her insignificant injuries whenever she'd asked. He had been a good man and would have made a great king. It wasn't fair! There were so many things he'd never get the chance to experience. He'd never marry, never have children, never live to old age... He didn't even get to say a final goodbye!

What made it worse was the knowledge that Edson hadn't wanted to go on this mission in the first place. As part of their studies, royal children in Livania studied records of the words of Riaas going right back to the first word received by her great-great-grandfather, which was that "those with the healing gift should never leave the safety of Livania's borders." Edson believed this word and had balked at Father's request, but Father made him go anyway. And, wherever Edson went, Geraint went too. So, Father had had a hand in killing off her two favorite people in the whole world! She blamed him for this. But Anwen would never voice those feelings out loud.

Growing up, Anwen quickly learned that any complaint about Father, or his actions, no matter how small, was met with a swift caning to her hand or backside. And speaking up for those whom she believed were not being treated right came with other consequences, like being shut in her room for a full day with no food and only water to drink and guards at her door or having her books taken away. One time, Father had her maid and guards temporarily replaced with strangers, people she didn't know, who treated her coldly on purpose. She had learned through these rough experiences to mask her feelings.

If anyone knew of her thoughts now, they would be shocked. If Father ever suspected the depths of her anger, her feelings of *rebellion*, she'd probably get thrown into the underground cells along with those poor clergy from the temple. Rubbing her arms to dispel the crawling sensation under her skin, Anwen shuddered.

Mother turned her way with a questioning frown. "What is it?"

"Nothing, Mother." Anwen tried keeping her tone neutral, but it was hard. Mother never took her side, so how could she think Anwen would confide in her now? She loved her mother, but they weren't close. She wished they were.

Maybe it was unfair of Anwen to expect anything else. Mother didn't have an easy task, walking a delicate tightrope as wife to an ambitious and aggressive king. Mother's name was Lethe. Father, who was easily exasperated or annoyed with her, had a way of lengthening the long "e's" in her name. He made it sound like she was his child instead of his wife. Anwen only hoped she wouldn't be forced into such an unpleasant marriage of state. Another shudder went through her. As the heir apparent and as a mere female, an arranged marriage might be much closer than she had ever thought, whether she wanted it to be or not.

It still begged the question of why there was a clear foretelling about Livania and Karpydosa being allies. Would Edson's death bring both kingdoms closer? She knew that Edson had been heralded a hero over there after Prince Jurem was brought to a full recovery.

Was she meant to marry Karpydosa's crown prince? She frowned and picked at a loose thread on the sleeve of her black dress. She'd never met the prince and didn't know what he was like. Not that that would matter. Alliance marriages were meant to join countries or families together, the feelings of the individuals were considered unimportant. She supposed she would be lucky if she were to marry someone of an appropriate age, as not every such marriage worked out that way. But was that even likely? She did know that Father hated King Marin, always spouting how he was such a greedy windbag. Father usually punctuated his comments with colorful language, and none of it was appropriate for a princess to repeat. Well, all she could think was that it took one to know one. She sniffed.

Squeezing her hands together, Anwen sighed. Her future marriage was in her father's hands. There wasn't much she could do about it. So there was no point in worrying. Maybe it didn't really matter anymore anyway. The only man she'd ever really set her heart on was Geraint, and he was dead.

Tears gathered in the corners of her eyes, and her throat closed over. She reached for her hanky and pressed the cool lavender-scented linen to her aching eyelids. At least he wouldn't have to watch her be married to someone else. That is, if he'd cared for her as much as she had for him. She suspected that he had, though he had never indicated it to *her* in any way. Anwen wiped carefully at the hot tears spilling down her cheeks. At least she was allowed to cry without being questioned about it.

Geraint had been good-natured and handsome. As her brother's boon companion, he'd always been around, even living as part of the family. She'd soaked up every quick smile and easy laugh, even if they weren't intended for her. Sometimes, as she grew into a young woman, she'd caught him glancing her way. Unfortunately, it had never been advisable or safe to pursue any kind of relationship and so she had never asked him about his feelings for her or dared allow herself to share hers with him. She hadn't even discussed the possibility with any of the young ladies of the court she spent time with. As Princess Anwen, she had been intended for a far more important marriage, after all, and he was intended to devote his time and energy to Edson.

There were eyes everywhere in the castle and plenty of wagging tongues, and even one inappropriate word would have gone around in a flash. But gossip never seemed to get around to her. Mother made sure of that because, when Anwen was younger, she hadn't always known how to watch what she said. She'd sometimes trusted the wrong people, which had gotten her and Mother into trouble with Father. And, whoever she was trying to help would get into trouble too, which inadvertently caused a great deal of discord among the servants.

Was it only a week ago that Edson's body had been brought back to Livania, sealed inside a massive casket? Time had stopped having meaning for Anwen. It sometimes crawled by slowly, the day never-ending, and then she'd blink and an entire day would be lost. Her body had turned sluggish and her brain foggy. She had heard that time would heal a broken heart and crushed spirit. There didn't seem to be enough time in all the world to heal hers.

When Edson's body had been returned, Anwen hadn't understood, at first, why it was only his. How she'd wished she could've seen Geraint one last time to say goodbye. But when she and Mother had gone outside to the enormous pavilion erected in the courtyard, she realized exactly why. In spite of the banks of flowers piled high, the strongly scented herbs scattered over the stones, and the scented candles burning at the head and foot of the sealed box, the miasma of death still lingered. They weren't going to look at Edson's face one last time. And knowing that he was inside that awful box in such a state made his death, no, *their* deaths, even more horrible and unfair.

Only one day had been granted for the court and the people to pay their respects. After that, the massive casket had been buried in the royal burial ground. And, to honor the other Livanians killed that day, there had been wooden plaques inscribed with their names and dates set up along one side of the pavilion. A portrait or bust for each of the deceased nobles and merchants in the delegation had also been on display. But the soldiers and servants had none. Their families would have to content themselves with empty graves and fading memories.

Anwen was feeling completely wrung out in every way. She constantly mourned the loss of Edson and Geraint. She'd loved them both like brothers when she'd been small. But, as she was growing up, she'd loved Geraint secretly in a daydreamy romantic way. Even though Anwen was now embarrassed at her younger silly self, she'd never stopped loving him, and her feelings had only grown stronger as she'd grown up.

How would she go on without either of them? They had been a constant in her life. The few weeks that they'd been gone had felt so empty. But she'd had their return to look forward to. Anwen hadn't ever imagined not seeing them again, and nothing could have prepared her for that awful news. Her breath hitched as she clutched the armrests of her smaller throne-like chair for strength. Mother placed a hand on top of hers to offer comfort and support. Anwen let out a shaky breath. She understood that Mother meant well. But there was such a chasm between them, just another thing that was mostly Father's fault. She might not agree with her parents on how they conducted themselves or treated others, but she understood that they were grieving too. They had lost a son. Her father had lost his heir. She resolved to try and be a little more sympathetic.

Anwen didn't want to be crippled by this terrible grief for the rest of her life. She had loved her brother and loved Geraint. She missed them and would miss them always. But she would have to find something to live for, a reason to wake in the mornings and get out of bed. She was the heir apparent now, and she would have to learn how to rule.

There was definitely an important meeting going on inside the small withdrawing chamber. Anwen and Mother didn't need to see Father or any of the merchants and nobles to know that. They could feel the electric tension as soon as they entered the large hall. The carved wooden door was close enough to the thrones that they could occasionally hear the rumble of voices behind it, interspersed with brief silences and exclamations.

The door opened, and Captain Arten and two guards left the inner room in a hurry. For a brief moment, some of the men's voices were audible enough to pick out words like "betrayal" and "war." Who had been betrayed, and what war were they discussing?

The two women let the captain and his men pass without demanding an explanation because, whatever it was, it seemed urgent. All the other men would have to enter the great chamber when leaving the inner room and walk right past them. And that was precisely why Anwen was sitting here silently waiting beside Mother. They were both determined, and, on this point, they were in agreement. They would insist on being told exactly what was happening. Right now, as soon as the meeting had ended.

When Edson was alive and the crown prince and heir, Anwen had accepted the fact that she was not included in royal affairs, but that was not the case anymore. She was now the heir apparent, and she would have to persuade Father to include her. She had every right to be informed of what was going on in the land she would someday rule.

The door finally opened, and men began filing out, talking in raised voices and gesturing at one another. It sounded like everyone wanted to be heard, making it impossible to understand what they were saying. Mother and Anwen stood up as one and slowly approached the knot of people. Once the men began taking notice of the two women, their voices started trailing off until there was an uncomfortable silence.

A moment later, a tall, thin, weary-looking man exited the inner room and stepped into their midst. His head of gold-blonde hair was unmistakable. For a couple of heartbeats, Anwen thought her eyes were deceiving her. Her heart stopped, and her vision narrowed into a tunnel focused on his face. "Geraint?

Is it truly you?" Clapping her hands to her heart, she swayed and nearly fell. Mother grabbed her arm and shook her. A muffled sound was coming from her mouth, but Anwen couldn't hear what she was saying through the roaring in her ears.

Anwen gasped in a huge breath and choked out, "How?"

Flitting across the very familiar face of Geraint with his pale-green eyes was a storm of emotions. Yes, he looked gaunt, but it was still him. He swallowed hard. "I'm so sorry, Anwen. I tried to save him."

Anwen jerked her arm from her mother's grasp and rushed forward. Pushing past those in her path, she hugged him, squeezing fiercely. Geraint grimaced, and she quickly released him. "Oh, I'm sorry! Are you hurt? Did I hurt you?" She mindlessly began patting his chest and face while repeating over and over, "How? How?"

"It's only my arm. It's healed but still a bit tender." His mouth twisted into a lopsided grin as he stared at her face, which must have looked quite frantic to him. "Don't worry. My arm is going to be alright."

Getting her wits about her, Anwen asked, "What happened? I thought everyone was dead! They told us you were all dead!"

"It's kind of a long story. I—"

"Daughter, Lord Geraint will need time to recuperate. I'm sure you can catch up with him later." Father's icy tone brooked no argument.

Anwen took a few steps back and mentally shook herself, embarrassed by her public performance. She quickly curtsied to Father, as did Mother, hiding her emotions from him with the dip of her head. Did Father always have to speak to her like he would a child, and *here* in front of the kingdom's most influential and powerful people? She hoped that her lapse in decorum, and her father's attitude toward her, would be overlooked in light of the traumatic circumstances that had befallen them all.

"What news is there, Your Majesty?" Mother piped up in a quiet voice.

"The news, dear wife, is that Geraint is alive, as you can see for yourself. He has just informed us of the true circumstances of our son's death. He has borne news of King Marin's duplicity and of his treachery. Now, if you would so kindly leave us to our planning." Father looked sternly at his wife and daughter, turned, and strode away with his men at his heels. Geraint nodded with a look of regret and followed after them.

THE NOVICE

The shock of seeing Geraint alive, then being summarily dismissed by her father, left Anwen shaken and feeling a little sick. Something in her father's voice and in his face had been so stony and cold, more so than what she was accustomed to. She didn't know how to feel. Everything was churning, making it hard to breathe.

Anwen turned to Mother, only to realize she was standing alone. Mother was quietly withdrawing after the men, which left her with a deep wretched sadness. She knew her mother put up with a lot from her father and had hoped to offer some commiseration, if nothing else. Watching her walk out the door made her think that perhaps they would never be able to share their feelings and would never be close or even friends.

Father did almost nothing where Mother was concerned. He didn't even show her the respect she was due as queen and the mother of his children. He could have tried harder. He *should* have tried harder.

Anwen sighed, and her shoulders sagged. It looked like persuading Father to include her in state affairs would never be a reality. And how would she handle her feelings around Geraint now that he was back? She was relieved to have him back but feared things would get more complicated. If only she didn't feel so powerless to do anything about her future.

Chapter 12
Ruthless Revenge

AT LAST, ANWEN HAD found him. Geraint was sitting on the stone ledge of the balcony alcove, staring into the distance at nothing. This balcony had a private view of the castle courtyard, so no one below could easily see anyone who might be sitting up here. Anwen hadn't come this way these past two weeks, not since they'd received the devastating news of Edson's and Geraint's deaths. It had been too heartbreaking to come this way, knowing she would never again see them filling the space with their voices and antics. Thankfully, that was no longer true of Geraint. She'd only been able to walk this way again these last two days, hoping to find him here.

I've probably worn a groove here. I've looked so many times, she thought wryly. Like one of those moths that can't stop circling a lantern.

Every time she passed by without seeing him, she'd counted the minutes until she could walk by again the other way. Geraint and Edson had loved this secluded balcony and spent a great deal of time here brewing up mischief, reading, or playing games. Anwen knew he'd be unable to resist coming here. She'd looked in other places but pinned most of her hopes on this one spot despite how unbearable it was to see it empty. Other than getting intermittent glimpses of him at mealtimes down the table from her, she hadn't seen him at all, and certainly not in private. Of course, it would never be the same without Edson, but having Geraint back from the dead made her grief a little less overwhelming.

Anwen quietly stepped into the alcove, her heart pounding so loudly that she was sure they would hear it down in the kitchens. Not wanting to take any chance of being observed from the courtyard, she kept well away from the railing. Anwen waited for Geraint to indicate that he knew she was there, but he made no move to speak to her. Either he was deeply lost in thought or not interested in acknowledging her presence. Well, no matter, she wasn't leaving.

Clearing her throat delicately, Anwen waited. And waited. Finally, she plucked up the courage to speak. "You know, I stopped coming this way after hearing... after..." She couldn't bring herself to say it. Taking a steadying breath, she continued, "I couldn't... It was just too hard."

Silence.

Holding on to that tiny spark of courage, she blurted out, "I came to see you."

Silence.

Sighing inwardly, she tried once more. "You can't blame yourself for Edson's death. I know you did your best. That's all anyone could ask."

In one swift turn, Geraint was on his feet and towering over Anwen, his pale-green eyes like shards of glass, his expression savage. She winced, bracing herself for whatever came next.

"You don't know that! Were you there?" His voice was intense, not loud, but so laced with emotion it cut like a knife.

Without skipping a beat, Anwen replied, "I know you, and I know you would lay down your life for my brother. That's enough." Her voice, thick with emotion, sounded like a stranger's.

Geraint's eyes were filled with rage and anguish as he looked deep into hers. Perhaps he was looking for answers. But then his face abruptly hardened. "Well, I didn't, and it wasn't enough." Stepping back and sweeping out a hand, he added, "I'm still here, and Edson isn't."

"But... but that wasn't by your choice." Anwen wasn't sure how to respond to Geraint's pain. He couldn't be blaming himself, could he?

"No, it wasn't." Geraint turned away from her and sat back on the ledge, facing the courtyard.

"Well, I'm glad you came back. I couldn't bear losing both of you," Anwen said very quietly and in a gentler tone.

Her heart thudded painfully behind her ribcage as she waited for him to reply. She gripped the edges of her full black sleeves so tightly that the braided trim dug into her fingers. But still, no reply came. Well, so be it. Anwen would try again tomorrow. Perhaps Geraint would be more open to talking to her then.

IT FELT LIKE IT WAS her hundredth time passing by the deserted alcove. The last three days had been long ones and a replay of Anwen's earlier search. She finally had to accept the fact that Geraint didn't want to be found, at least not by her. She'd persisted because things were happening in Livania, and the one person who would perhaps speak to her about them was avoiding her. She assumed all the recent activity had something to do with the "duplicity" that Father had mentioned but being left in the dark meant she didn't know what to think and was completely unable to do anything about any of it. It was frustrating and unfair. As the heir apparent to the throne of Livania, it should *not* be this way!

Anwen was getting desperate. Where was that infuriating man? Where could he possibly be hiding? She'd searched everywhere she could think of, including the attics. But there were no footprints in the dust on the floors up there, so she hadn't ventured further into the dark, cobwebby, and cavernous spaces. She'd thoroughly investigated every other corner of the entire castle, even though the sight of every single place where she, Edson, and Geraint had ever played or worked had caused a fresh wave of grief to wash over her. Her brother's absence had left a huge hole in her heart, and she missed him so much that sometimes she didn't know how she kept breathing. Now, not being able to speak to Geraint, knowing he didn't want to speak with her, added to her pain. Grief, frustration, and annoyance churned inside her, keeping her from eating or sleeping properly.

Sitting on the carriage block in front of the castle main doors, Anwen determined that today she would find that man, and nothing would stop her.

The castle and its grounds weren't so extensive that finding someone would be impossible, even a certain someone who didn't want finding, and, throughout her childhood, Anwen had had plenty of practice finding people. She felt a fresh wave of grief as she remembered how Geraint and her brother used to try and hide from her younger girl-self. Sometimes they wanted to do "boy stuff," but they could never evade her for long, despite their best attempts to hide. Anwen was surprised to find a tiny smile forming as she remembered their indignant shouting and complaints at her popping up in the middle of their games. She knew this old pile of rocks better than anyone else alive and certainly better than Geraint.

Where could that confounded man be? She had to have missed somewhere. Unless Geraint was staying in his room... She paused, tapping her chin. For obvious reasons, it was not an option to search through men's rooms... Though, if she was careful... No! What was she thinking? She indulged in a ladylike snort and shook her head. There was no way he was hiding in there anyway. He would never be able to stay still that long. But, there was one place he might be, the royal stables. Even though she'd searched there before, perhaps she'd missed him that time, or else he'd just been clever at hiding.

Jumping to her feet, Anwen dusted her hands off and headed across the yard. It was time for a showdown.

And that is where Anwen finally found the proud, brave, and enigmatic Lord Geraint, crouching like a naughty little boy in the stall of his favorite horse, a blue-roan stallion named Dusk. The exceptionally loud greeting she'd received by Lenart, the head stableman, had been a dead giveaway, especially as it had been directed away from her, toward the back of the stables. Lenart was not a subtle man.

"Well, hello, *Lord* Geraint," Anwen said, emphasizing his title. "Fancy seeing you here. Are you enjoying the ambiance?"

Still kneeling in the straw while pretending to tie the laces of his boot, Geraint snorted dismissively. And, being an agreeable sort, so did Dusk.

Holding back an unexpected laugh, Anwen continued with her formal tone. "Is that any way to greet your princess?"

Geraint rose in one fluid motion to his full height, looking a little sheepish and rather annoyed. Dusk yawned, quite unimpressed by the whole performance unfolding before him.

In an extremely controlled and formal voice, Geraint replied, "Greetings, Your Highness. And, what may I do for you this fine day?"

Switching from her formal tone to an angry one, Anwen replied crossly, "You can stop avoiding me, for one."

"Obviously, it didn't work, because here we are," Geraint said, shrugging and turning one hand palm up.

"No, it didn't. I can be very determined when I want something. Surely, you haven't forgotten *that*." Anwen folded her arms and tapped her foot.

Geraint quirked an eyebrow at her but didn't otherwise respond. It was such a familiar expression of his that it was hard to ignore. But she pressed on.

Switching back to her formal voice, Anwen said, "You have options today." Taking her time and wanting to make him squirm, she pretended to flick dust off her left sleeve with her right hand. Straightening her spine, she continued, "Now, My *Lord*. We can have this discussion right here, with the head stableman, the grooms, the stablehands, and all the horses listening in, *or* you can accompany me for a walk around the formal garden. The apple trees are in bloom. They have a much sweeter smell than the stables."

While Anwen spoke, Geraint stood with one eyebrow raised, his shoulders back, and arms folded. It had always been a weakness of hers when he lifted that damnable eyebrow of his. She wanted to either kiss him or punch him. She wasn't sure which. If only he'd stop it with that eyebrow!

As soon as she'd finished speaking, he unfolded his arms and said silkily, "As you wish, My Lady Princess." Geraint gave his best court bow, complete with turned calf and simpering expression. He then indicated the stable door, making a flamboyant gesture with his arm. "After you."

Anwen spun around and began marching down the alleyway of the large stone stables. She hadn't gotten far when she heard Geraint mutter under his breath behind her, "Meddling nuisance." Her lips twitched into a satisfied smirk, which he couldn't see. He could only see her very straight back as she purposefully led the way to the formal garden.

Walking the newly graveled garden paths under the heady fragrance of apple-tree blossoms on a sunny spring day seemed so normal and perfect. But there was really *nothing* normal about it. Anwen had never walked anywhere alone with Geraint. He had been Edson's companion, not hers, and they were the ones that had always been together. She was the one who had been the odd one out, only a visitor to their games and studies. And it wasn't perfect either because, although it could have almost felt romantic despite the vastly formal distance between them, there was an oily dark shadow of grief and betrayal chasing any possibly fluttery warm feelings away.

Aware that saying the wrong thing could shut Geraint up like a tight lid on a jar of preserves, Anwen chose her words with great care. She was counting on three things to soften him up and make him answer her questions: their childhood friendship, her appeal to the goodness of Geraint's heart, and his insatiable curiosity. In a measured voice, Anwen said, "I need your help." It was the first thing either of them had said since leaving the stables.

Watching Geraint clench and unclench his tanned hands, her stomach tightened, and she waited. Not wanting to lose what little ground she had gained, she resisted trying to force a response. Sometimes staying silent was the most convincing argument.

Finally, Geraint spoke after what felt like years of waiting. "I'm probably the last person you should ask for help." He shook his head and glanced over at her. "I was no help to Edson."

Anwen's veil fluttered behind her as she walked, and she carefully let out the breath she'd been holding while he spoke. "Hmm, well, you're the only person I can ask. In fact, you're the only person who is likely to help me."

For one long moment, Geraint turned, giving her his full regard. There was no way that he could see her eyes under her lowered eyelids. He wasn't anywhere near close enough. It was just as well. She didn't want her eyes to betray how much he affected her. She couldn't allow anything to distract her. She needed to concentrate on what she would hear. And she needed to think about what she would say next.

A gardener was weeding nearby, so Anwen walked on a bit further before speaking again. The garden wasn't large, so they moved slowly along the crisscrossing paths, sometimes going in a different direction past the same sections. The castle was built up against a mountain, so the ground was rocky. All kinds of decorative plants were growing in raised garden beds filled with soil, and various trees were planted in trenches or holes, some of which had taken weeks to dig out. Anwen knew this because she spent a lot of time out here and often would see the gardeners at work.

Once they had again moved out of earshot of the gardener, Anwen said, "Father doesn't tell me anything, and if there's gossip to be heard, it's never spoken where *I* can hear it." Why did everyone treat her like she couldn't handle the truth? It was most frustrating.

"Hmm. I wonder why," Geraint said in a gently mocking voice.

"What is *that* supposed to mean?"

"It means, Your Highness, that you are known to meddle after jumping to conclusions. It usually gets you, and also those who spoke to you, into trouble."

"If you think all I do is meddle and cause trouble, then maybe I don't need any help from you!" Clenching her hands at her sides, Anwen fumed and then sighed miserably. "What good am I allowed to do? What difference can I make to anyone? I might as well have been born a cat! All that's expected of them is to sleep, purr, and scamper about, amusing people in exchange for food."

Moving closer and bringing his head near hers, Geraint said solemnly, "They're also expected to make kittens."

Anwen stopped short and folded her arms tightly around her middle. Geraint came to a halt beside her. Glaring at him, she said, "Yes, well, I suppose I should be grateful for such small mercies."

Geraint began to laugh from deep inside his belly. It was so familiar, rich, and rumbling and had such happy feelings attached to it that somehow it made Anwen really smile. It was the first time she'd heard him laugh since he'd left, and she'd missed it. Of course, he'd been completely unlike himself since he'd been back, and this was the first glimpse he'd shown of his old self.

Shaking her head, Anwen looked at the toes of her shoes and hoped Geraint would decide to speak honestly with her. Perhaps considering her troubles could help him forget his own for a little while. She gave an exaggerated "hmph" that lacked any ire and began walking again.

Geraint moved up to remain in step with her, tucking his thumbs into his belt. Anwen could tell he was wrestling with himself because he huffed and sighed several times. Finally, he looked up from the path and said, "I'm sure no good will come of my speaking, but what exactly do you want to know?"

Yes! Sweet victory!

Remaining poised while inwardly jumping up and down with anticipation was extremely difficult, but Anwen clamped down on her feelings to appear completely calm. She was sure the only things giving her true feelings away were her shaking hands and flushed cheeks. She couldn't do much about her coloring, but clutching her sleeve edges helped somewhat with the shaking. Not wanting Geraint to notice her excitable state of mind, which might cause him to clam up, she replied as calmly as possible, "I have two questions for you. Firstly, what exactly happened the day all of you were attacked, and secondly, what is Father planning to do about it?"

Anwen knew what she was asking wasn't anything more than what was already known to the men in Father's circle *and* probably their wives, mistresses, business partners, and horses too! When would Father widen that circle to include her? Anwen sharply cut off *that* particular train of thought. She needed to concentrate on whatever answers Geraint was willing to give her.

Geraint stopped walking and pinched the bridge of his nose. "This is exactly why I've been avoiding you."

Anwen stopped beside him. "What do you mean?" Exasperation leaked into her voice.

Geraint looked steadily into Anwen's eyes before speaking again. "I didn't want to have to tell my story again and relive that day." His voice sounded heavy as if the words didn't want to leave his tongue. "It was a horror, and nightmares still plague me. I'll never forget what happened, but I truly wish I could."

"I'm sorry, Geraint. I really am." Anwen wished she could say something, anything that would make things easier. She hated this. "But you truly are the only person I can ask. Believe me, if there was anyone else, I would..." her voice trailed away, and she looked miserably into his pinched face.

Even though Geraint had been back nearly a week, he still looked as gaunt as the day he arrived. It was clear that he wasn't sleeping or eating well, and there were deeply gouged lines around his mouth and eyes that hadn't been there before he left. Weeks! That was all it had been. When he'd gone with the others, it had been the start of spring. Now it was the middle of spring. How much could things change in such a short amount of time?

Geraint's obvious deep distress was why she wasn't going to ask anything else, even though she badly wanted to know about any possible plans for the ceremony acknowledging her ascension as the new heir to the throne. And it was because of a silly ceremonial observance that no one had time for and why Anwen, unfortunately, had no official status and, therefore, couldn't find out the things she wanted, no, *needed* to know. But official or not, it shouldn't block her from knowing Father's plans or finding out what had happened to her brother. She desperately hoped Geraint would tell her. If he wouldn't, well, then she was out of possibilities.

As if Geraint had heard her thoughts and knew just what she needed to hear, he said, "Look, I'm sorry. You have every right to know. Being officially the heir or not, you *are* the heir." He paused and swallowed hard. "And you're Edson's sister. He loved you, you know, even though he could never resist teasing you."

Anwen felt tears gathering in the corners of her eyes, and a lump formed in her throat. A breeze ruffled her veil as she waited for him to continue.

"The only thing that kept me alive and fighting to get back to Livania was needing to tell the story for Edson's sake. He would have wanted everyone to know what happened. I'm sure he'd want you to know how his story ended."

Anwen let out a slow breath. Finally, she was getting somewhere.

Geraint motioned with his hand, and they began walking again. "But," he said and paused, "I'm going to tell you a much shorter version. You don't need to know every gruesome detail."

Anwen slowly nodded as they strolled down a path they'd been down at least twice before. They turned abruptly yet again to avoid the gardener, their feet crunching on the fresh gravel.

Once they were out of earshot, Geraint continued, "Edson realized we'd been betrayed. It was the last thing he shouted before we began fighting for our lives. I guarded him as best I could, and we both fought hard, back-to-back, the way we'd trained together. But we were completely surrounded and completely outnumbered. Our betrayers spared no one. It was only by some oversight on their part that I survived."

Anwen felt as though she'd been stabbed in the heart. She'd known there was some kind of betrayal when she'd overheard it spoken from the withdrawing chamber and again afterwards when Father had mentioned the king's duplicity, but hearing it from Geraint confirmed her worst imaginings. Treachery from someone they should have been able to trust, and had trusted, while on a mission of mercy!

"But, why? Why such a betrayal?" Anwen could barely choke out the grief-stricken words. "What... what did they hope to gain by killing Edson?" Her grief suddenly turned to anger. "He was there to help them!"

"That's the crazy thing. I overheard a Karpydosan say that the spoils belonged to the mercenaries. *Everything*, except for Edson's opal." Geraint shook his head slowly, opened his mouth to speak, but clamped it shut again.

"Why the opal? Doesn't King Marin have enough gold to buy all the opals he could ever possibly want?" Geraint's story simply wasn't making sense. No one would do such a thing, would they? Did King Marin murder her brother for a piece of rock?

A fresh wave of anguish and horror swept through her. For a moment, Anwen wanted to sit down right there and then but sternly took hold of herself. She had wanted to know and had demanded Geraint tell her. She'd best prove to him right now that he hadn't made a mistake, or she knew she would never hear another word.

As he glanced her way, Geraint frowned. His expression held concern.

Anwen straightened, lifted her chin, pulled her shoulders back, and attempted to hide her trembling hands by gripping the edges of her sleeves. She mustn't lose control now. She had to show that she was strong enough to hear the truth.

Geraint studied Anwen's face and nodded. "Exactly. I couldn't figure it out because it made no sense, but one of the Livanian merchants in the council meeting told us all a tale about gems of power being mined in the Southern Island kingdoms. He thinks King Marin was hoping to gain Edson's healing power by acquiring the opal."

He wiped a hand down his face, and his voice turned sorrowful. "Edson wore it the whole time we were there. And you know he had the habit of constantly running his fingers over it when he was healing someone. He used to say that the smooth texture helped him to concentrate."

Anwen did remember. But, since when did an unconscious habit get a person killed? Anwen twisted her fingers together, trying to prevent her hands from shaking again.

The answers she'd demanded were more distressing than she could ever have imagined. Edson, oh Edson, how horrible. He didn't deserve what happened! He was trying to help. Who just murdered someone like that? Over a stupid necklace! Healing was no secret. It was openly available, sometimes for a fee, and it definitely wasn't something Livanians were trying to hide. What kind of person planned murder like that? Her thoughts were going in circles, making her angrier and angrier.

Clenching her hands into fists, Anwen demanded, "Why didn't the king just ask about it? It makes no sense!"

"People like that are never satisfied with what they have, so it doesn't need to make sense," Geraint grumbled. The discontent in his voice sounded as if he had a few people in mind. Her father could easily be one of them. Geraint continued, "Even if he had asked, there was no reason for him to believe Edson's answer. But he probably didn't want to tip us off about his intent if the opal was the source of Edson's power."

Her brother's life was stolen for no good reason! And all those good and loyal men slaughtered with him. Anwen almost wished Geraint had refused to tell her, but she felt relief now that she finally got some answers. It helped to know the truth, even if it was only to learn the deaths of Edson and the others were a senseless waste. "So, now what?"

"Now we seek revenge," Geraint's voice lowered, and Anwen felt a shiver run up her spine at its sudden ice-cold and malevolent timbre.

Rubbing her arms at his ominous-sounding words, Anwen steadied her voice and asked, "What will that entail?"

Geraint didn't answer right away. He looked at Anwen in a way that made her very afraid that he wouldn't tell her anything more. She held her breath and tried to keep her expression calm.

Seeming to come to a decision, Geraint said bitterly, "Well, we can't invade Karpydosa. Not only do they outnumber us, but they would also have the home ground advantage if a war came to their land." He paused and clenched his hands. "So many times I've pictured killing King Marin with my own two hands. If I could, I would. And his son too, if he had anything to do with it, or even if he only knew and failed to warn us," Geraint snarled, and his pale-green eyes turned stony.

In a low voice, she didn't recognize as her own, Anwen asked, "Do you think Prince Jurem knew and said nothing?"

"I don't know. I hope not." His voice was grim, and he shook his head. "We thought of him as a friend. We both *liked* him."

"So, we can't go there, and we can't kill Marin. How are we going to get revenge? I don't understand what we can do from here that would hurt him or his kingdom."

"We're going to hurt the Karpydosans by going for their people here in Livania."

Anwen was still confused. "But aren't they just innocent people?"

"You see! This is why you don't get included. You think like a little girl and not like the heir to the crown. King Marin can't be allowed to get away with this insult and treachery or he'll try something worse next time. He has *got* to pay for his crime." Geraint slammed his fist into his hand. "When King Marin starts losing his people here, and their goods are seized, there will be an outcry in his own kingdom. He'll have to face his council and his people. If there is any justice, then he'll lose his crown or his head." Geraint smiled, but Anwen knew there was no humor in it.

"But, won't he retaliate?" A cool breeze off the mountain stirred the air, smelling like pine forest and rain. As Anwen put a hand on her head to hold her veil in place, she felt cold and shivery all over, picturing innocent people being murdered by soldiers.

"He can try, but we're preparing for that. It's why I'm still here. I'm just waiting for the go-ahead." His expression was hard and set.

Not sure if she wanted to hear the answer, Anwen asked in a slow, cautious voice, "So, how are we preparing?"

"We are making access into Livania as difficult as possible. As we speak, fishing villages along the Bay of Brothers are being evacuated, the docks are being demolished, and the largest rocks possible are being dumped in the water to make beach landings difficult. Extra walls and watchtowers are being built while the old defensive ones are being fortified. And, the bridges across the Amesvar have already all been destroyed."

"In less than a week?" Anwen was staggered. How could this be happening?

"Well, building things takes more time than destroying things, but our soldiers, and our people, are enraged." Geraint sounded proud of them. He added in a grimmer voice, "Having their much-loved crown prince murdered will do that."

Chapter 13
Cat without Claws

TWO DAYS HAD PASSED since their walk in the garden, and Anwen had spent the time fretting and pacing. They hadn't spoken further, as Geraint had occupied himself with preparations for the imminent eradication of Karpydosans on Livanian soil. Anwen, appalled by both the plans and his approval of those plans, had not sought Geraint out. She sometimes wondered if she would ever want to speak to him again.

Father was behaving like a mad boar, so she was avoiding him too. When seated on his throne, he would fasten his bloodshot and enraged eyes on anyone who entered the room. He was a terrifying presence, not sleeping, roaring orders, and drinking far too much. The atmosphere at the castle was roiling, coming closer and closer to boiling over. It was as if the people she'd known her whole life had become complete strangers.

What could one princess, one small cat without claws, do against the coming horrors? She didn't know. She felt too helpless to try and do anything, but she couldn't just sit by and do nothing! So she paced and discarded one idea after another.

Well, she'd begin by trying to visit the servants of Riaas in the castle cells. Anwen didn't know what she might be able to do to help them, but she had to see if there was something. There was no way she'd ever be allowed to speak to them, so she would have to sneak down. After giving it some thought, she decided it would be best to go after supper as most of the castle corridors would be empty by then. She knew she would have to slip by the guardroom at the bottom of the stairs to ensure no one saw or heard her. That was the only way to guarantee no word made it back to Father. She shuddered to think what might happen if he ever found out.

Those poor people had been on her mind since hearing that Father had had them arrested. They'd been seized three weeks ago inside the temple, thrown in chains, and brought to the castle. Anwen had heard the commotion outside but had been unaware of what was going on out there until she'd looked down into the courtyard from the privacy of the balcony alcove. She'd been horrified to see people shouting, making threats, and even *throwing things* at the dozen elderly-looking clergy in torn and dirty white robes on the two wagons. Unable to believe her eyes, she'd watched them ordered to climb down from the wagons and then be roughly herded by armed guards towards the enormous main doors.

Wanting to see what would happen, Anwen had immediately run down to the cleverly concealed little door leading to the minstrels gallery overlooking the main hall. Upon opening it, she'd crept into the deserted space beyond. She crawled on her hands and knees through the heavy draperies that separated the performance balcony from the stairwell and small storage space. It was particularly stuffy back there. Well, it had been ages since there'd been music in the hall, so the dust and stale air were no real surprise.

The acoustics in the large room carried every whispered sound down to the floor and up to the gallery, so Anwen had to be extra careful to be quiet. She held her breath and peeped between two banners hanging over the balustrade. She couldn't risk getting caught. She'd for sure be locked in her rooms on dry crackers and water rations if she was. She stifled a sneeze and froze in terror. Had anyone heard?! She peeked again and realized no one could possibly overhear her with all the noise down at floor level.

Shocked, she'd watched Father and the men in the hall roar abuse, insults, and threats at the small group of clergy standing before them. Their response had been to stand quietly with their heads bowed, not reacting in any way.

Unable to force herself to watch for very long, Anwen had slowly and carefully exited the gallery, then bolted through the deserted hallways back to her rooms. Slamming the door, she leaned back against it. Her entire body was trembling, and she began to cry.

Anwen would have never believed it if someone had described either scene to her. Livanian citizens – some she had known her whole life – were behaving like barbarians in the very courtyard of the castle and the main hall! It shook her sensibilities, and her innocent belief that Livanians were all good decent people was stripped away forever.

Father had boasted and laughed about it to everyone in the great hall later that night at dinner. He even had some of the ordained dragged in, including the high priest and priestess, making them kneel in front of the head table on the stone floor. Arlo had also encouraged everyone present to taunt and jeer at them. It had been terrible to watch, and to see people – previously such courteous and formal people – descend to such actions was extra frightening. It was the first time Father had ever done something like this, but sadly, it wasn't the last.

From then on, the atmosphere in the hall had changed. The women and children stopped coming to sit at the long tables at dinner. Father didn't seem to notice or care that his wife and daughter were also absent. Uncouth men, mostly strangers, now filled the benches as they banged their tankards on the tables and shouted curses and blasphemy. Anwen had sometimes listened just out of sight of the open doorways to glean information, but after a couple of close calls, she became frightened of being caught and stopped. It upset her to discover there were more evenings when Father had made the clergy part of the dinner entertainment.

Even Mother admitted that he'd gone too far. Strangely though, afterwards, she'd become increasingly silent. It was unlike her. When Anwen saw layers of bruises peeping out from under her long black sleeves, she suspected she wasn't hearing everything that was happening and was sure she didn't want to. Perhaps Mother had finally stood up to father, but it was clear as to who had won.

Anwen had no concrete hope as to what she might accomplish by sneaking down to the cells and no real hope of success, but the clergy were good people. They didn't deserve what was happening to them. She couldn't just leave things the way they were. She'd have to at least try!

The first and only time Anwen had seen the prison cells under the castle was as a child. Father had taken Edson and Geraint down on an "educational tour," and she'd tagged along. The cells were rarely in use, and even though they held no prisoners that day, they were still nightmarish. The place had been dark and damp, reeking of rot, mold, and overlaid with the eye-watering stink of rats. The place had frightened her, and she'd tried to forget it even existed.

The idea of going down there again gave her ice-cold sweats. Anwen didn't have much stomach for human misery, but there were innocent people down there suffering while she slept in a clean bed each night after a comfortable supper. She didn't know if she could help them but knew she had to try.

Waiting in her quiet chambers, Anwen gulped, remembering the smell. This time she would bring along a cloth scented with mint oil to wipe under her nose, something she'd read about in a book of practical nursing from the stillroom. She hoped that would help keep her stomach under control. Throwing up at the stench of rats, human waste, or whatever else she might come across would not be helpful. And she didn't want to add the stench of vomit to the prisoners' suffering.

Anwen waited until after supper and after the servants had brought hot bath water to her rooms. The maids then left her alone for the evening, and the castle became quiet. They wouldn't return until later to bank up the fire in her sitting room and take the bath water out. And that would only be when she turned in for the night, giving her at least two hours. With any luck, she'd be back well before then. If she wasn't... Well, she couldn't bear thinking about that.

The influx of crude strangers, who previously would *never* have been given any service or welcome in the castle, also meant that the castle corridors were no longer altogether safe, especially after dark. Her heart was hammering in her chest when she finally left the safety of her rooms.

On her way to the cells, Anwen took a quick detour. There was always food left out in the kitchens for those on night shift duty. Doing her best to go unnoticed, she reached around the corner and dumped an entire bowl of cheese biscuits and a smaller one of little sweet cakes into her canvas shoulder bag. If nothing else, she hoped to offer a bit of comfort in the way of food to the prisoners.

Edson had once told her that getting away with mischief was much easier if you looked like you were on an errand and needed to be somewhere. Anwen took that advice to heart and strode boldly through the corridors, nodding confidently to the few people she met. No one even acknowledged her as she passed by, and she began to feel more certain of success. Anwen was relieved to discover that the hallway leading to the broad stone stairs and lower levels was deserted.

Unsure if the stairs to the cells were guarded, Anwen cautiously descended. Guided by the dim light of lanterns hanging at infrequent intervals on either side of the steps, she watched and listened carefully, but there wasn't a soul to be seen. Relieved, Anwen slipped down into the gloom. As she silently approached the guard room at the bottom, she could smell stew and hear several voices in a muted conversation. The door was partly closed, and she drew a shaky breath before flitting across the opening.

No one had seen her! Shaking with nerves and terror, Anwen carefully walked down the corridor, trying to stay next to the stone wall without actually touching it. She was sure it would be cold, wet, and slimy. On her left were empty cells, their barred doors hanging open.

Where were they?! Anwen knew they had to be down here somewhere. She didn't remember the corridor running on very much further. They had to be here. There was simply nowhere else in the castle to house a group of prisoners.

There was a sudden scrabbling noise and a frantic scurrying in front of and over her feet. Anwen strangled a scream before it left her throat. That would bring the guards down on her like hounds on a rabbit. The additional shock of nearly stepping on a rat made her head spin. She clutched her head, waiting for the dizziness and sudden thumping in her ears to subside.

Anwen stayed hunched over, head still spinning, as she gathered the courage to continue. She had never felt so sick and afraid and never wanted to give up on anything so badly in her life.

Drawing together her shattered resolve, Anwen straightened and silently mouthed, "I am a Princess of Livania. I am going to do this. I'm not going to run back to my room like a coward." Her lips trembled, and she was shaking uncontrollably, but she somehow found the courage to take another step and then another. Haltingly, she walked on.

Oddly, the smell grew worse the further she went. The thick greasy scent of human waste now overlaid the stench of rats and mold. Gagging, Anwen fumbled out her mint-scented cloth and took a few breaths through it. She'd never much cared for the smell of mint, but now she was grateful she'd remembered that particular trick. Anwen rubbed the cloth under her nose and carefully took a breath without it. Good, the scent remained strong even when she didn't breathe directly through the fabric.

It seemed like miles but was actually only a dozen feet before Anwen came to a turn in the corridor. As she moved around the sharp bend, she finally discovered the clergy in a wide cell at the end of the passage.

Anwen would remember the next half hour for the rest of her life.

As she approached the barred doors lit by lanterns on the opposite wall behind her, Anwen could see the shapes of bodies sitting against the cell walls and a few lying on the damp dirt floor. Several were muttering prayers while someone sobbed softly. Another voice was murmuring words of comfort. A low moan from one of the prone bodies made her shudder, and she gripped the canvas strap of her bag with her sweaty hands. Anwen tried to speak and found herself unable to make a single sound. She gulped, nearly choking on the thick atmosphere.

Anwen stepped closer to the cell. After a few careful shallow breaths, she managed to whisper, "May I please speak with High Priestess Celeste or High Priest Dante?"

An old priest, sitting and staring into space just beyond the bars, slowly turned his head in her direction. Anwen had the uncomfortable feeling that he didn't really *see* her. He nodded vaguely, slowly rose to his feet without saying a word, and shuffled toward the back of the cell. Anwen gripped the strap of her shoulder bag even tighter as she waited, praying there would be no delays. She knew she wouldn't have long and wanted to be done and gone before being discovered.

Suddenly, High Priestess Celeste stepped out of the darkness. The two lanterns on the wall behind Anwen provided just enough light that she got a good look at Celeste's face. She was horrified to see a badly scraped cheek and a black eye. Her once beautifully upswept silver hair that Anwen had seen and marveled at as a child was now roughly bundled into a ragged knot at the back of her neck and her long white robes were torn and stained with dirt and blood.

"High Priestess!" Anwen struggled to speak clearly past the lump in her throat as she quickly gave a bow with her head.

"My dear child. Please, just 'Celeste' will be fine." Every softly spoken word sounded like it was a huge effort. "We have no time or need for titles here. There is a great deal we need to say and only just enough time to say it." Celeste paused, sighed, and rubbed her forehead. "We have a word for you, in fact, several words. That is not the usual thing, but these are not usual times. Not for us, not for you, and not for Livania."

Anwen felt somewhat shocked and blurted out, "Words? You can give words outside the temple?" Anwen herself hadn't been to the Temple of Riaas for years, not since the days when Father had brought the family with him, wishing to be seen as a good family man and beneficent ruler. She had never received a word, but then, not everyone did.

Celeste smiled slightly and gave a little nod. "Yes, the words of Riaas are as true here as anywhere. People seem to feel that words spoken in the temple carry more weight, but that's not true."

Just then two dark shapes emerged slowly from the shadows to stand beside Celeste. It was High Priest Dante, being supported by another shorter priest. Celeste turned to her husband and put an arm around his waist. "You should have continued resting," she murmured just loud enough for Anwen to overhear.

Dante struggled to stand a little straighter and quietly replied in a raspy voice, "No, this is too important. We both need to be sure to deliver these words." He turned to the man supporting him and said, "Thank you, Jerome." The man nodded and stepped away.

Celeste gripped her husband tighter when he began to sag to one side. Dante placed one arm around her shoulders for added support and held the bars with his other hand. Anwen could see that two of his fingers were bound together with a stained rag, and she shuddered.

Anwen could see that Dante was unable to place barely any weight on his left leg, and, as he turned to the light, his face showed signs of blows. He had a split lip, and several bruises bloomed darkly over his forehead, cheek, and jawline.

Dante turned toward Anwen, his blue eyes shadowed by pain and determination. "You and I have not spoken since you were a little girl." He coughed a little, and it sounded wet. "I am High Priest Dante, but we will not stand on ceremony here. You may simply call me 'Dante.'" His voice was weak, not quite a whisper, but far from the clear tone she remembered.

It sickened her to think that Father was responsible for their injuries. She then remembered the rolls in her bag, and her stomach sank. A bit of extra bread couldn't possibly make any difference to their suffering. Her gift was nothing. She was nothing – a cat without claws. No, she wasn't even a toy stuffed cat! Useless. She was useless.

Anwen felt the tears gathering at the corners of her eyes, and she blinked hard. "I'm sorry for everything. Are you being fed? Do you have enough water?" She pressed her lips together to prevent them from trembling. This was not the time to start crying. She could at least listen without making a fool of herself! She gave herself a mental kick.

Celeste sighed again and replied, "We are being fed and have water. Some of the guards are... Well, let's just say some of them are unkind, but not all of them. And we could use a healer's help, but we won't be sent one before the end."

Anwen felt a chill go down her spine, and she swallowed the sour thickness that rose in her throat. "The end?"

Dante coughed and replied quietly and soberly, "Yes. We've known our end was near before we were seized in Tilmar. But that is of no importance. Now we must give you the words of Riaas entrusted to us as time grows short."

Dante coughed again, a rattling cough, and continued in a slightly choked voice, "Firstly, the cat without claws will make her mark. In three times one hundred years, those marks will be seen."

Anwen was confused. How could he know what she called herself? And what did he mean by three hundred years? She'd be long dead in three hundred years!

"Secondly, things in Livania will continue as they now go. The river has changed its course and *must* flow in its new bed."

Anwen stepped up to the bars and gripped them tightly. "Things must continue? Do you mean even after Father is gone? But why? Why can't they go back to the way they were?"

Celeste "hmmed" softly and reached between the bars, lightly touching Anwen's shoulder with a hand that bore scrapes and broken nails. "We cannot explain, my dear. That isn't how it works with the word. But I will tell you this much. The actions put in place by your father, the king, will have a long-lasting effect. You cannot stop what is happening and what will happen. And furthermore, you must not try."

"Celeste," Dante frowned at his wife and continued, "Say no more. You know we do not interpret the word. We only pass it on to the recipient." He turned to Anwen and said sadly, "However much I wish we could."

As Celeste looked at Dante, she also frowned. "I think, in this case, I am not wrong to offer a little more." She pursed her lips and added, "But you are quite right. I must be cautious, and for that reason, I will keep my advice to the minimum."

She turned to Anwen and said, "Lastly, through coveting an opal, harm has come. Yet from *another* Opal, healing will come." An odd look crossed her face and she stopped speaking. Suddenly, she asked, "How is King Arlo?"

Anwen, concentrating on the third word given her, snapped back to the conversation. She sucked in a deep breath without thinking and nearly lost the contents of her stomach from the taste of the fetid air. She swallowed thickly, concentrating on breathing in the scent of mint until her stomach calmed.

After letting go of the bars, Anwen wrapped her arms around herself and tried to think of a safe answer. Well, she had to trust someone, and there was really no point in trying to deceive. Settling on answering as honestly as possible, she replied, "He's not well. I don't know what's wrong with him and neither does Mother. He's become a stranger to us and a frightening one."

Looking down at her feet, Anwen said, "When news of my brother Edson's death came, it changed Father, made him harder and colder." She looked up and grimaced. The clergy had experienced his cruelty firsthand and more than once. "But when news of King Marin's betrayal came, it was as if something snapped inside him and something dark has overtaken him. He drinks more and more, refuses meals, and even refuses to sleep. He surrounds himself with strangers, men from the streets, mercenary soldiers, men who would *never* have been offered service in the castle before. And now he's willing to take revenge on more innocent people, this time on all Karpydosans in our kingdom. I overheard one of the servers from the hall tell Cook that he's even planning on selling people into slavery!"

Anwen took two more shaky breaths before continuing, "Mother thinks he needs a healer, but he refuses to even consider it. The last time she brought it up to him, he struck her in the face and knocked her down. He threatened her with imprisonment if she so much as whispered the word 'healer' in his presence again. Mother and I don't know what to do." The last sentence came out in a rush. Anwen hadn't been able to tell anyone about Father *striking* Mother. Despite the circumstances, she felt relieved at being able to tell someone.

Dante nodded. "Your father makes his own choices. And, you must make yours."

Anwen slowly shook her head. Sometimes it didn't feel like she had *any* choices. "What am I supposed to do when I have no power, no influence? I can do almost nothing."

"Do you truly wish to help the people being hunted and killed in your kingdom?" Dante's voice seemed even more strained, and his breathing sounded more labored.

"Yes, of course," Anwen said without hesitating.

"While your father sows death, you can spare lives."

"But how?"

"Captain Arten has a sympathetic ear and enough rank and influence to be able to take action," replied Celeste. "He will be your ally. Ask him to find farmers to take in and hide the children caught in the king's war. Farmers are your best choice because they will be further away from the turmoil and prying eyes. Farm families are large, and no one pays attention to children."

"How do you know this?"

Celeste smiled sadly and replied, "We are Servants of Riaas. He speaks to us. Not all words are meant for others. We receive them too."

Hearing Celeste's comment completely stunned Anwen. Her heart began thumping in her ears, getting louder and louder with every second. Anwen felt as though she were going to pass out. "But if he speaks so clearly to you, then why did you give my father such a misleading word? You could have prevented all of this!" Anwen's voice started to rise. "My brother would still be alive!"

Celeste replied sharply, "Dante told the king to heed all past words, but he did not. Even his son warned him, but he would not listen. Willful ambition and greed have caused him to walk this path out of the many available to him."

Her anger rising, Anwen said, "I still don't understand why you didn't explain everything to him as you have to me. I just..." She clenched her fists at her sides. "I just don't understand why Edson had to die! And so many more people will too. And I can do nothing about any of it."

Anwen closed her eyes and clenched her jaw, willing the tears of frustration and anger back. She would not cry, not here!

When Dante coughed again, Celeste gently laid her wrist and then her palm against his face. "You're running a fever, my dear one," she murmured. Dante turned his face, leaning into her hand, causing Anwen to feel that she shouldn't be watching such an intimate moment.

Dante sighed, coughed softly, and spoke again, "Time is drawing short for us, Princess Anwen. And, it's growing short for many other people too. Don't dwell on the might-haves, should-haves, and could-have-beens. Focus on what you are able to do. You are responsible for your choices and your actions. Your father has chosen his road and is determined to walk it no matter what. Time is also running out for him."

Dante stopped speaking. He looked steadily into Anwen's eyes, seeming to consider for a moment before continuing, "It's not too late for Lord Geraint. Help him see past his guilt and his pain. He will need your strength and friendship upon his return."

Celeste drew a sudden breath and said, "We are out of time, my dear." She briefly looked between the bars back the way Anwen had come. "You must go now before the wrong person discovers your presence here. Remember our words and do your best to follow them. Study the words of the past. Also, remember that Riaas is eternal, even if his priests and his temple are not."

Anwen's feet felt glued to the spot as she struggled to process everything she'd heard. Suddenly, she remembered the bag of rolls. Quickly pulling it over her head, she pushed it through the bars into Celeste's free hand. "Here are some fresh rolls I stole from the kitchens. I hope you and the others will enjoy them."

Immediately Anwen felt like the biggest fool in the world. She stammered, "I'm sorry. I'm so sorry. The rolls are stupid. They won't help. I wish..." Her words trailed off. Not knowing what to say or do and frustrated with herself, she momentarily squeezed her eyes shut.

After passing the bag to Dante, Celeste quickly reached through the bars to grasp one of Anwen's cold hands. "Shush, shush now. It's alright, dear. Please don't worry." Celeste squeezed her hand while giving it a gentle shake. "Thank you for the rolls. It's a kind gesture, and we *will* enjoy them. You are a fine brave young woman, and that courage is going to save lives now and in the future." She gave Anwen's hand a final little shake and released it. "But you must go now and quickly."

Dante spoke up one last time. "Thank you, Anwen. Remember the words of Riaas. And may he watch over you and yours from now until forever. Now go and don't look back."

Realizing it might be the last time she saw them, Anwen looked deeply into their eyes and said, "Goodbye." She managed to get the word out clearly before her throat clogged up with unshed tears. She turned and began walking back along the corridor, concentrating on putting one foot ahead of the other and *not* on looking back.

Anwen quickened her pace while trying to remain silent. Thinking straight was impossible with the pounding of her heart and the thoughts whirling around and around her head. She stopped just shy of the guardroom door to listen. It remained partly closed. She could hear the low tones of conversation and the rattling of dice. As she rushed past the doorway, she heard a gravelly voice shout, "Hey! Someone's out there!" Anwen didn't pause. Instead, she took off as if she'd been launched from a slingshot.

Running like demons were pursuing her, Anwen fled up the dimly lit stairs, praying that there were no guards at the top. She could hear pounding boots behind her. Wearing only light shoes, and carried by a wave of terror, she outdistanced them until her toe caught on the top step. She landed hard on the smooth stone floor with her hands and knees and skidded half her body length down the hall. Anwen had been far enough ahead that she might've escaped, but then she got caught up in her skirts.

Strong hands roughly grasped her upper arm, pulling Anwen upright and jerking her around to face her two pursuers. "Hey there! What do you think you're doin'? You can't be..." Anwen found herself staring into the faces of two very young and very surprised guardsmen, one of whom was also very familiar. "Anwen? What in the seven unholy hells are you doin'?!"

Anwen didn't know whether to feel relieved or not. Tall blond Glen was Head Stableman Lenart's youngest son. Anwen had spent her childhood racing ponies against him and losing as often as not.

Feeling angry after the intense emotions she'd been experiencing, Anwen exclaimed, "None of your business!" Her hands and knees were also stinging from the fall, so for good measure, she added, "And that's Princess Anwen to you!"

Glen looked rather nonplussed, but at least he let go of her arm. "Your pardon, *Princess* Anwen. But you haven't answered me. Nobody's allowed down there. And how did you get down there anyways? Me and Jake are goin' to have to take you into custody."

Oh, no! That was the last thing she wanted. Thinking fast, she straightened her spine and said in an authoritative voice, "I am the heir to the throne of Livania. There should be no secrets from me. I merely wished to ascertain that the prisoners were being treated humanely." Would an arrogant attitude do the trick? She hoped so because, otherwise, her life was going to become very difficult.

Glen pursed his lips as he looked at her for a long moment. "I can't say that them priests are being treated well," he said slowly. "But me and Jake here try to make sure they get enough water, and we wheedle extra bread and things from the kitchens for them. Some of the others... Well, let's just say I don't think it's right to treat folk that way, especially innocent folk."

Scratching the short hairs on his chin, Glen looked at Anwen and frowned. "We're supposed to be runnin' you down, you know, and takin' you to our shift captain. He was the one who shouted when he saw your shadow pass across the doorway." Glen exchanged glances with Jake, who didn't look happy. "The thing is... The shift captain... He's not a nice man."

Jake took a breath and muttered, "I think we searched the closest corridors and didn't find no one, Glen. We looked and listened, and the only livin' thing we saw was that big black tomcat what comes down to hunt rats."

Glen nodded and looked directly at Anwen. "I think that's exactly what happened, Jake. Not a soul in the corridors. Musta' been the cat runnin' past the door that made the shadow and any noise Captain mighta' heard."

Anwen knew a cue when she heard one. "Thank you," she said quietly. Nodding gratefully at both of them, she took off at a fast walk down the hall. Before turning the first corner, Anwen could hear Glen and Jake loudly declaring that the black tomcat was the only living being anywhere nearby as they descended back down the stairs.

Once safely back in her rooms, Anwen bolted the door and sank to the floor. She felt shattered. After resting briefly to try and quiet her violent shaking, she hurried to eliminate all evidence that she had even left her couch that evening. She couldn't risk being caught now.

Stripping off everything she was wearing, Anwen tightly bundled her clothes and shoes into an old blanket and shoved it into the back of her closet. She would dispose of them on another day. She then went into her small bathing room and got into the tub with the now lukewarm water. Using a spicy mouse ear soap, Anwen quickly scrubbed herself from head to toe. She was grateful that the skin on her palms hadn't broken open when she fell, and she was sure the soap would remove any hint of stench from the cells.

Still terribly keyed up, Anwen got dressed in a loose robe and knitted slippers, sat on the small chair in front of her mirror, and carefully began combing her hair with hands that wouldn't stop trembling. As she worked out a knot, she reflected on the extraordinary run of luck she'd just had. Even being caught by Glen and his friend Jake had been lucky. She hoped their shift captain believed their story, but even if he didn't, there would be no proof that she, Anwen, had been down to see the prisoners. Not even the ordinary canvas bag she'd left behind could be, without a doubt, connected to her.

After combing her hair, she twisted it into two long braids. The task was unexpectedly calming. If anything, *anything* at all had gone wrong tonight, Anwen would now be sitting in a cell or trying to explain her actions to Father. She shuddered, imagining how that would have gone.

But it had been worth the risk. And she'd received not one but *three* words from Riaas! How extraordinary! Not only that but she'd also been given some advice. Even Dante seemed to break the hard and fast rule about giving interpretations. Everything they'd said was burned into her memory, but she'd also write it all down as soon as her guise of "I've been here all evening" was complete. It was hard to believe she'd only been gone less than an hour, and it was quite early. Still, she didn't want anything to be out of place should anyone come asking questions.

Sitting at her little writing desk, Anwen selected a pen, opened her ink, and carefully wrote out the words of Riaas. She then hid the page in one of the books on her shelves. Once that task was complete, she returned to her desk and considered for a moment, tapping her pen on her lower lip. Anwen didn't know Captain Arten all that well, and she didn't know if he was on duty that evening. But even if he weren't, she could at least set her plans in motion, and with that in mind, she carefully composed a short note to the captain.

Peeping out her door, Anwen saw a male servant coming down the hallway carrying a tray. She called him over and asked him to deliver a message for her. It seemed like only a few minutes before a soft tap on her door signaled that a reply had come back. And just like that, she had a meeting with the captain arranged for the following morning.

Immediately after reading the captain's reply, Anwen felt utterly drained, as if everything got wrung out of her. She'd been running on nervous energy since reaching her rooms, and she simply had nothing left.

Anwen slipped the reply under some papers in a desk drawer and dragged herself over to her bed. Crawling under the soft woolen covers and pulling them up to her ears only reminded her of how wretched the cells were. As the events of the evening replayed in her mind, Anwen started shaking again, her earlier terror echoing through her body. Sorrow, pity, regret, and guilt overcame her as tears wet her pillow. She felt helpless and afraid that nothing she could do would actually make a difference. Poor Dante. Poor Celeste. She remembered Celeste's attempts to comfort her and cried harder. Even when facing imprisonment and certain death, the priestess had wanted to help.

Once she'd cried herself out, she fell into an exhausted yet, somehow, still uneasy sleep. The usual shuffling noises of the servants coming and going on the other side of her bedroom door and other nighttime sounds of the castle went unnoticed.

Chapter 14
Meddlesome Maiden

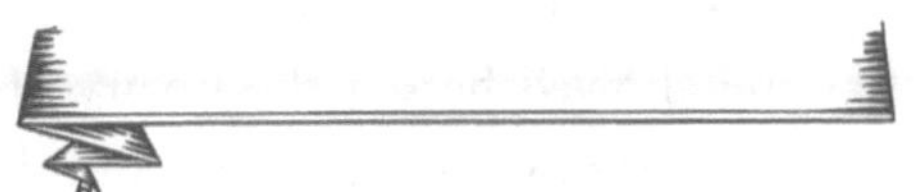

EARLY THE FOLLOWING morning, Anwen found herself studying Arten's impassive face. Despite having slept badly from being chased by terrible dreams, she managed to arrive at their meeting on time, and she hoped, looking competent and calm. He was seated opposite her in the small private study beside the library. She poured out two cups of tea and offered biscuits and cheese while pondering the best way to open a discussion involving such a sensitive, no, *not* sensitive; a discussion involving such a *traitorous* subject.

Once again, deciding there was no point in trying to deceive and that she had to trust someone, she merely asked Arten for his help. Her request clearly surprised him, but once Anwen had described her visit to the cells and outlined her hope of saving as many children as possible, his surprise turned to something akin to respect, and he agreed.

Arten proved to be an able conspirator. He quickly and easily fleshed out the bare bones of the plan Celeste had suggested, adding several refinements that Anwen herself would never have thought of. By the time Captain Arten took his leave, Anwen felt, for the first time in weeks, hope for the future.

Having defied Father by slipping down to the cells to speak to Celeste and Dante had been the single most terrifying thing she'd done in her entire life. Sitting in the clear morning light, she could hardly believe she'd actually done it. But upon further reflection, she realized that she felt different today. In doing what she thought was right in pushing through her fears, she not only found her courage but also felt much more confident. Now that she had a plan and some help, all she needed was the resolution to follow it to the end and maybe, just maybe, a little more luck.

Finishing the last of her tea, Anwen read over her notes. She stood, folded the papers, and slid them and her pencil into the secret pocket in her dress. She would put them with the rest of her private writings. At last, she had a chance to be more than a helpless pawn, more than a cat without claws.

Anwen moved toward the study door and let out a long sigh. It was going to be another long difficult day with all the turmoil still roiling through the castle. She twisted the doorknob, not yet ready to leave the privacy of the small room. She stilled her hand as she allowed herself the luxury of a wish. Imagining, for just a moment, that none of this had happened and that in a few seconds, Edson and Geraint would tromp past on their way to some amusement or task, and she could poke her head out the door to tease them. Anwen listened wistfully for any sound from the silent corridor but then gave herself a mental shake. There was no magic to make such a wish come true. She straightened her shoulders and smoothed out her expression before pulling the door open and walking through it with renewed determination.

THE NEXT DAYS WERE in some ways the most intense that Anwen had ever had. Presenting a calm and, in fact, a rather *vacant* face to the world was much more difficult and draining than she had anticipated, especially since she was also frequently exchanging notes with Captain Arten and had to conceal her rising excitement at finally making a difference. She had no other outlet to express her feelings, so she took to writing in her journal at every opportunity, her agitation and nerves finding their way onto the page. Anwen had always been indifferent at journaling, despite Mother's constant nagging, but had immediately come to depend on the relief she felt at writing it all down.

The captain had immediately snapped into action, knowing that any delay would reduce the success of the rescue plan. He organized pairs of men dressed in nondescript clothing to immediately ride out, in an unobtrusive manner, and quietly meet with farmers up and down Livania. The men were equipped with letters of introduction and small silver medallions cast with Arten's personal badge to prove that they were truly speaking for him. Some of the furthest outlying farms were unaware of their king's latest actions, but everyone had heard of the terrible loss of their crown prince and their king's revenge on the Servants of Riaas. Opinions were divided.

At first, some of the farmers who were chosen to receive messages were a little skeptical when told that children's lives were at risk, but the careful selection of those people meant that they not only trusted the messengers but also soon began to arrange safe houses and transport on their own, without further urging. Return messages had begun to come in almost immediately, and Captain Arten discretely passed news of them to Anwen several times a day, in the stables or hallways. They could not risk any meetings, but casual passing-bys were unlikely to be noticed or remarked upon.

Anwen's greatest fears that she would not be believed and would find no allies were now laid to rest. She had done what she could for the time being and she hoped that all these extraordinary efforts from so many ordinary people would be enough.

After having casually "bumped into" the captain yet again, Anwen returned to her rooms feeling tired and yet somehow exhilarated at the same time. She hung up her black cloak and sat down in a chair to remove her short boots. She sat quietly for a few minutes, lost in thought.

Having found success in her plan, Anwen didn't want to stop but she knew anything she did behind Father's back was dangerous. Anyone could report her actions at any time. If she wasn't cautious, if he ever found out... Well, in his current state of mind... she shuddered. The cells would be the least of her worries. Until she was formally declared the heir, she had no authority to say or do anything noteworthy or *anything* at all. She also knew Father didn't want any challenges to his plans, and he wasn't about to declare her elevation in rank any time soon. The few times he had mentioned her new title, it had been connected to finding her the "right" husband.

Anwen had always known she'd probably be sent into an arranged marriage with the idea of cementing some kind of alliance. What she'd never known was *what* kind of alliance or *who* she might have to marry. She'd sighed over it, of course, as any young woman would but had always accepted the idea as her duty. But, she'd been too young to take it very seriously, until now. Father was no longer the man she'd known all her life. Now, she didn't know and couldn't guess what he might be planning in his disturbed mind. Now, she felt a real danger in the idea of marrying his choice of man.

Impatient with herself, she yanked off her boots and let them thunk against the floor. It didn't look like she'd be free any time soon, not to rule anyway. But what had High Priest Dante said? Time was running out for Father. Considering the way he was burning himself out, she wouldn't be surprised if he would go into apoplexy during a fit of wine-fueled rage, and she was very sad to realize that she wouldn't be sorry if it happened. It was as though the father she had known, who had occasionally taken her up on his horse or pushed her on the swing in the garden, was dead already.

It felt like a storm was brewing, considering her father's erratic behavior and the events unfolding, and it was just a matter of time before the deluge hit.

She was right to be worried. The evil storm broke the following day.

Anwen and Mother were breakfasting early along with some of the court when Father unexpectedly swaggered in, accompanied by some of his men. The atmosphere immediately turned heavy and almost poisonous. After he'd demanded wine and food, Father banged his mug on the table and bellowed that he was done "coddling those useless priests" and that they would be hung at noon in the courtyard. His men had roared approval, and some of them had laughed.

A cold wave raced up and down her body and, for a few moments, Anwen feared her breakfast was going to come back up. She watched without really seeing as one of the women across from her snatched up her two children and fled the hall, but Anwen had been frozen in place.

At first, she was in shock, but then her mind began racing. She wanted to scream, throw herself in front of her father, and plead for mercy. She wanted to run down to the cells to see if she could stop the madness or, at least, say goodbye.

Before she could do anything at all, Anwen felt Mother's hand clamp down on her shoulder as she very quietly and firmly said, "No."

Anwen had barely turned her anguished eyes to Mother's face when one of the serving maids approached, holding out a sealed note. Anwen shook off Mother's hand, stood, and snatched the note before fleeing the hall. She could hear the rustle of Mother's dress right behind her, but as soon as she was around the doorway, she began to run. It didn't matter that running in the halls wasn't appropriate behavior and was sure to attract attention. For the time being,

Anwen didn't care about propriety. Running allowed her to get away from Mother and find a place to be alone.

The quickest and best choice was the balcony alcove where she'd spoken to Geraint after his return. She seated herself in the far corner in a spot not visible from the hallway. Anwen needed time to gather her scattered thoughts and to read the now crumpled note clutched in her cold fingers. Her hands were shaking with trepidation as she opened it.

At first, the blocky handwriting was unfamiliar, but soon she discovered that it came from Glen on behalf of Dante. Dante thanked her for her kindness and urged her to remember the words she had received, encouraging her not to worry for their sake. He went on to assure her that there was nothing more she could've done to help them, they had known their time was coming, and they were all at peace.

Glen added a note at the bottom. He regretted informing her that two of the frailest ordained had passed away in the night, succumbing to their injuries. Also, his squad had received a reassignment, and he feared that it meant the execution would be in the next few days.

Tears welled in Anwen's eyes. Glen had wanted to warn her ahead of time. He certainly hadn't known that the delivery of his note and the order of execution by Father would happen simultaneously. She felt the tears as they began running down her cheeks. She shoved the note into her pocket, burying her face in her hands, allowing the grief to overtake her.

At noon, which came far too quickly, Anwen watched helplessly from above as the hastily built gallows in the courtyard were soon surrounded by a crowd of people. She could hear cheering and shouting, but others stood silently watching, only present because they'd been forced to be there by circumstances beyond their control. All too soon, the Servants of Riaas were marched out to stand and await their demise. She noticed their numbers were fewer with two not having made it this far.

The first five climbed up the stairs and stood quietly in a row as their "crimes" were read out for all to hear.

Anwen simply could not watch anymore.

Whirling blindly, she buried her face in her arms against the back wall. A sudden bang and a roar from the crowd told her what was happening. By then, she was sobbing so hard she didn't hear when it happened a second time. She slid down the wall, huddled on the floor, and cried until there were no more tears left.

Wracked with shudders, Anwen eventually stood. She wiped her tears with her sleeves and pulled a handkerchief from her pocket for her nose. As she walked slowly back to her rooms, she felt numb in every way. After taking a sleeping draught, she went to bed, not wanting to think or remember anything for just one evening.

The following morning, still feeling sluggish and numb, Anwen returned to her observation post on the private balcony. She was grateful and relieved to see no evidence of yesterday's executions in the courtyard below. Instead, milling around were Father and his men of war.

According to a note from Arten, delivered to her along with her breakfast tray, this crowd was only a portion of the sword-wielding men who would ride out to wreak havoc on more of the innocent citizens of Livania. Others were gathering in other places. She'd also learned that Royal Decrees had been sent the day before to the mayors throughout the land stating that the "good loyal" citizens of Livania should round up all "traitorous foreign" Karpydosans and bring them bound to the town squares and city centers. Those same mayors were to divide up and distribute any properties owned by the Karpydosans as "they saw fit." This sinister addition to the decree was supposed to be an additional motivator. *But nothing ever goes to plan.*

As Anwen watched them form into companies and ride out, her numb emotions gradually came back, and she became increasingly distraught at being unable to stop the madness. She saw that Geraint went with them, leading his own company alongside King Arlo's command. According to Arten, Geraint was heading to the City of Tilmar and the towns around it. Others were heading to other cities further away and their surrounding towns. Anwen hated seeing Geraint's determined face. She'd sent him a note two days before, asking him not to shed the blood of innocent people. He hadn't replied.

Once Father and most of his men were absent, the women and children returned at mealtimes to the long tables in the great hall. Those men who stayed behind were castle guards, staff, and those too young or old to fight. Mother and Anwen took their seats at the head table. Mother insisted they present a united front to provide "leadership" and "boost morale." Anwen disagreed, but she knew better than to show her disapproval. Father would be told if she refused to do as she was instructed, perhaps not by Mother, but surely by someone else attempting to curry favor.

Anwen received her first anxiously awaited letter from the captain two days after the men had ridden out. It had arrived only an hour before the evening meal, and the maid delivering it to her had raised an inquisitive eyebrow at the masculine handwriting. Anwen had blushed a bit, knowing that there would no doubt be a new set of rumors circulating through the castle, but she also knew that speculations about a sweetheart were much better than the truth.

After reading the letter several times, she'd concealed it between the pages of a rather boring book of poetry. She'd placed it among her other books on a shelf in the sitting room. There was an open window nearby. The evening breeze had picked up strength, blowing one of the curtains against the closest books, so she closed it before leaving her rooms.

To keep up with appearances, Anwen had then dragged herself off to dinner. Now she was seated beside Mother, taking tiny bites and pushing the rest of her meal around her plate. The effort of listening and responding to the inane conversations around her made her stomach twist even more.

Finally, Mother turned her way and asked, "Are you not well, daughter? You have hardly touched your dinner."

Taking a moment to try and think of an acceptable answer, Anwen grabbed her silver cup and took a sip of wine. She nearly choked, but quickly recovered, pressing her napkin hard against her mouth. She needed to satisfy her mother, and not alert anyone else who might be listening. "It's nothing, Mother. I'm just tired."

"Oh, well, alright then." Mother daintily dabbed at her lips with her linen napkin. "You may retire early to your chambers. I can always send for a healer if you need one."

"Thank you, Mother. But that won't be necessary."

Once she was back in her rooms, Anwen began to pace. Before dinner, there'd been a breeze blowing, but now the wind was howling with a mournful sound. The heavy blue curtains helped block out any cold air seeping through the closed windows, but she shivered anyway.

Anwen stopped pacing and retrieved the book of boring poetry from the shelf in her sitting room. She lit the lamp on the small round table beside the couch and sat down. A fire was burning brightly in the hearth before her, but it failed to warm her body or cheer her spirit. Her hands began to shake as she took out the folded paper. Unfolding it, she began to reread the words on the page.

The falcon flies like a deadly arrow toward the sunrise.
Striking down all manner of starlings in those skies.
A wide net is cast, catching the sparrows.
They alone are saved from all deadly arrows.
The hawk and the falcon fly swiftly together
Nothing now stops them, not even bad weather.

As she studied the words, a gust of wind suddenly hit the windowpane, making it rattle hard. The unexpected noise startled Anwen, making her jump, and she pressed the letter against her chest. There was no need to study the letter any further. She knew it off by heart. At first glance, it was merely a fanciful poem in rhyming couplets about birds. But she knew the poem was bearing terrible news.

Before leaving the castle, Arten had explained how to decode his letters. He knew it was best to take precautions as there was no way to safeguard messages completely. He had chosen different birds to represent people and had given her a list. For example, he was an owl, Father a falcon, and Geraint a hawk. The foreigners were starlings, and the foreign children were sparrows.

Her imagination had filled in any blanks after she'd read the poem several times in its entirety. According to the letter, the evil "storm" had now released its full fury. Reason and kindness had fled from the land. As the chaos spread, many "good" citizens of Livania were taking advantage of the king's decree for their own gain, overpowering and imprisoning any and all foreigners, regardless of whether they were Karpydosans or not, visitors or citizens. They also killed some "accidentally" ahead of the king's men arriving. Since Father was out for blood, he didn't care how it happened, so long as the job got done.

As part of the king's command, the captain was able to ensure foreign children had a chance for survival. Arten had fellow officers and loyal men in different companies aiding the cause. They were doing their best to keep their men in line while as many children as possible got "lost" in the confusion and found their way to safety. Commander Balcom, aware of this, was happy to turn a blind eye. Anwen was grateful to discover that not everyone was a monster like Father. And Father, who had a permanently crazed look about him, did not notice what they were doing through the haze of alcohol and bloodlust.

Anwen put the book away with the letter safely tucked between its pages. She blew out the lamp before heading to her bedroom and climbing into bed. Overcome by grief, she cried into her pillow until sleep finally claimed her. The wind continued blowing, and she slept fitfully, chased by unseen terrors through murky dreams.

Two more days of fretting, pacing, and eating little had passed before Anwen received a second letter. Mother had finally sent a healer, but the healer found nothing physically wrong with her. Anwen still missed her brother and explained that his death was the reason she was out of sorts. At least seeing the healer had satisfied Mother. After that, Anwen was left alone, and she could read the latest update in peace. The letter carried a mix of good and bad news. The good news renewed her belief in Geraint. Anwen happily reread the part where Geraint changed his mind and became one of Arten's allies.

Yesterday, the hawk had a change of mind,
Remembering the virtue of being kind.
Turning to the owl, he now does as he should,
Using his eyes and wings for the greater good.

Her third and last letter arrived the afternoon before her father returned. In that letter, Anwen read how much the falcon enjoyed swimming in the blood of the starlings. She hoped it was only a metaphor. But even if it was, it was still an ugly fact about the man who had sired her. He was enjoying the suffering he was causing and, even worse, the bloodshed of innocent people. Father was destroying the lives of the citizens he'd sworn to protect, and the welcoming reputation that the Kingdom of Livania had built over the years with other kingdoms.

Anwen threw herself upon her bed and cried into her pillow. A short while later, she sat up, wiped her face, and blew her nose. She was tired of crying, tired of grieving. Tears had become part of her everyday life since hearing that Edson and his delegation were all dead. She rested her aching head on her hands and allowed her thoughts to wander.

Why did these two kings have to be so horrible? She promised herself that one day when she was queen, she'd be fair and generous. She would do her best to be a protector of her people and her kingdom. Until then, she would just have to endure. Endure and persevere. Releasing a huge sigh, she rose and went to change her crumpled dress before continuing with her day.

Later that day, one week after having ridden out, the man who wore her Father's face arrived back along with his men. Those soldiers who had ridden further away would only be returning in the next few days.

Hurrying once again to the balcony alcove, Anwen had a private view of the courtyard below. It seemed like everyone had come out to see the men return. There were a few women waving cloths from windows while people of import stood on the front stairs before the main doors. Others stood in the courtyard to welcome the men. She witnessed a mixture of emotions on the men's faces as they rode their horses past the cheering crowd before heading to the stables. Some men whooped and grinned along with the people like they had won a huge victory, while others looked grim, or haunted.

The cooks and other staff had already begun preparing for the "victory" feast. The king wanted a grand affair, so they didn't have much time to get things ready for the event set for two days from now. Anwen was sickened by the whole idea. Only a monster would consider the killing of his own innocent and helpless citizens and foreign visitors a "victory" worthy of a celebration feast. Anwen knew she would have to attend, but the idea revolted her.

Chapter 15
Discerning Destiny

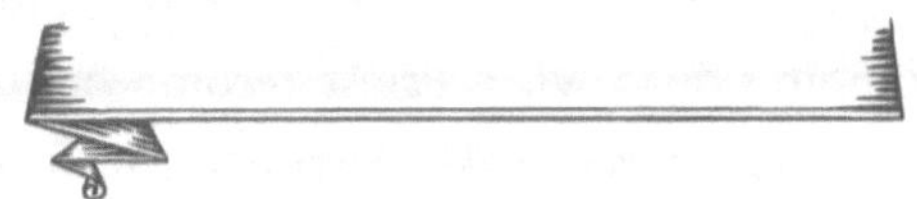

THE MOTLEY GROUP OF refugees had been journeying through Bariny for about three weeks. While traveling an uphill road, Amity was lost in thought, walking behind a cart fully loaded with cabbages and other vegetables. Thankfully, she hadn't been holding any of the children's hands at the time, although, if she had been, she probably wouldn't have been caught unawares. The load had suddenly begun to shift, and unexpectedly, cabbages began rolling out onto the road. Amity didn't notice until it was too late. The first ones tripped her, knocking her off her feet. She went down hard, getting pummeled by a few more. As soon as one person laughed, the others joined in until one of the adults put a stop to it. The humiliation felt far worse than the injuries.

While Amity's scrapes and bruises were getting attended to, a few people gathered the fallen vegetables, rearranging them on the cart and rebalancing the load by placing some into other carts. After that, Amity tried avoiding everyone, but the children were persistent as a swarm of bees that she couldn't outrun.

Proving the point, one little girl asked innocently, "Would you say that Fate caused you to get hit by cabbages?"

Oh, rats! Amity wished the ground would open and swallow her whole.

Oblivious to Amity's embarrassment, the girl plowed on. "Isla says that everything that is going to happen will happen. She says that's Fate."

Amity shook her head, gathering her thoughts while trying to decipher the child's question. The first thing that came to her mind, though, was to ask, "Who is Isla?"

Swinging her arms, the girl replied, "Isla is the lady who used to bring fresh eggs every morning to the monastery. She said she never had a husband or kids, so Fate gave her chickens instead."

Another child piped up, "I never liked Isla. She looked mean."

The first girl glared at the second girl. "She can't help how she looks! And we're told not to judge a book by its cover!"

"Oh, well. Uh..." Amity realized that she'd better respond quickly before things escalated. Grabbing onto what Priest Jerome had taught in class, she repeated his words, "Fate is for the weak. Destiny is for the strong."

"What does that mean?" asked the first girl.

"It means nothing," Paxton said loudly and angrily, as he and his friends caught up to Amity and the children.

Grubby goblins and *rats!* Amity was not prepared to handle Paxton right now. She was having a hard enough time as it was. Her mouth opened and closed, but no sound came out. Paxton smirked at her inability to speak. Why was he picking on her anyway? Over the past two weeks, he had constantly poked at her with unhelpful comments while calling her by that horrible nickname, "Ashes." What was he trying to accomplish by hassling her? She wasn't sure. And right now, she didn't care.

Deciding the best plan was not to respond to Paxton's prodding, Amity ignored him, focusing on answering the girl's question instead. Bending her head toward the girl, Amity explained, "It means that people who believe that everything is set by Fate will just let things happen, but people who believe in Destiny will try and do their best. If we all did our best, the world would be a better place."

"Pfft. Look how well that worked out for Jerome," snarled Paxton. Standing directly in front of her with his hands on his hips, it was clear he didn't intend to back off.

Amity clenched her hands and demanded, "Are you calling Priest Jerome a liar?"

The children stopped walking and watched the exchange with wide eyes and open mouths.

"Priest Jerome stayed behind with my grandparents and the others. They might all be dead by now! They might be *worse* than dead! What kind of destiny is that, huh?"

Amity's voice softened as she realized why Paxton was upset. "Whether they are or aren't, I don't think their lives have been a waste. They believed in their destiny, enough to be willing to face death so that we could live out ours."

Paxton didn't reply. Instead, he whirled around and stomped off, and Amity "hmmfed" under her breath. His friends hastened after him, glaring and muttering as they hurried past her.

Chapter 16
Feast or Farce

THE TWO DAYS PASSED more quickly than Anwen would have liked. The evening of the "victory" feast found her sitting before her dressing table looking into her mirror as Beitris, her maid, skillfully applied kohl to Anwen's eyes and colored creams to her cheeks to brighten her pale complexion. Beitris chattered about inconsequential things as she gathered Anwen's thick dark hair into a confection of braids and swirls. Dressing hair was a particular talent of Beitris'. Her mother, Jane, was Queen Lethe's maid, and she'd passed every bit of her talent on to her offspring.

As Beitris patted a braid into place, Mother unexpectedly swished into her rooms. Anwen watched with surprise in the looking glass above the vanity where she sat. What was happening now? Mother *never* came in before dinner.

Clasping her hands tightly in front of her, Mother smiled, although it looked somewhat forced. "Hello, my dear. I'm glad to see you are almost ready. As you well know, this victory feast is very important to your father. He will make a big announcement this evening and will be angry if anyone is late." Mother sounded like she was reading a part in a play, not like herself at all, and it left Anwen feeling unsettled.

Turning to Beitris, Lethe continued, "Please, ensure my daughter wears her best dress. The new one made last autumn."

While Mother spoke, Beitris quickly put the last pin in place and curtsied. "Yes, Your Majesty."

"But Mother," Anwen said, turning to face her, "we are still in mourning."

"Not for tonight. Your father wants a celebration, and you are to be part of it. Tomorrow, you can go back to your black." Her voice sounded bright yet brittle.

"Yes, Mother," Anwen answered reluctantly. There was no point in arguing. Father would get his way even if Anwen disagreed with him. This was *worrying* though. What was going on?

"Good." Mother twisted her hands together, her gaze drifting to Anwen's vanity table and the folded black veil resting on top. "And be sure to leave your veil behind."

Beitris would have pinned the veil onto her hair after she was fully dressed. Anwen held back her questions and objections, choosing to nod instead.

Mother's unnaturally stiff smile faltered, making Anwen feel a little guilty. But Mother quickly concealed her emotions by straightening her spine and firming her lips, and Anwen, as so often happened, stopped feeling sorry for her.

As Mother walked out the door, she turned and added, "I will be back very shortly to escort you to the hall."

The door shut before Anwen got the chance to ask why. Mother was acting so strangely. Anwen hadn't been escorted to dinner by Mother for years, not since she'd been small, and in fact, the last time they'd walked together was at Edson's funeral. Whatever Father had planned at the feast must require them to present themselves formally.

Anwen frowned and shook her head. Tonight's feast should be a time to hang their heads in shame, not to strut about with pride and fanfare. Anwen sighed, knowing she'd have to go along with whatever Father had planned or face the consequences.

Seemingly unaware of Anwen's feelings or perhaps determined to ignore them, Beitris returned from the wardrobe and said, "Here is the one your mother mentioned." She held out the richly colored silk dress. "I think it's the most beautiful thing you own, and it makes your eyes look even bluer." Her voice was warm and encouraging.

"Do you have any idea what this is all about?" It was doubtful her maid knew anything, but it didn't hurt to ask.

Beitris laughed self-deprecatingly. "Me? They never tell me anything for fear I might let something slip."

It was true. Beitris was too close to Anwen and known to be loyal, being of a similar age and openly friendly to her. Beatris would never be trusted with any secrets.

The dress *was* Anwen's favorite. It was cut simply and dyed a deep-sea blue with gold embroidered oak leaves along the front and down the sleeves. It looked beautiful on her, and Beatris was right, the color did bring out her eyes.

Anwen remembered the occasion it had been made for as if it were yesterday. It was the first time she'd had a new gown made for her as an adult, not as a young girl, and she'd been so excited. It had been the yearly feast held every autumn when foreign officials would visit Livania and join in the hunts for deer and boar. She'd turned many heads that day, but only one man had made her heart flutter.

She'd smiled and flirted a little, and Geraint had responded with a gallant bow and a kiss on the back of her hand. There was nothing about the bow or the kiss to cause any comment except that his hand had held hers a fraction longer than was necessary, and his usual, teasing self had turned a bit pensive. After kissing her hand, he'd raised his head, his eyes looking soulfully into hers. Anwen had felt a spark of connection between them, her heartbeat had kicked up a notch, and she'd sucked in a breath at his intense nearness. But then he'd laughed, dropped her hand, and spent the evening dancing with every other female in the hall.

To say it had been disappointing would be an understatement. However, Anwen only sighed for a few minutes knowing she was destined for an arranged marriage. There was no way Father would ever choose someone of Geraint's rank for her. She'd tried very hard not to think about that evening, and yet... But that was another time, and Geraint had been a different man.

Even though Geraint had returned three days ago along with Father, Anwen hadn't seen him since he'd left. It seemed like he was avoiding her again.

Beitris helped Anwen to dress, careful not to let the gown snag on the hair she'd so artfully braided and pinned. Next came the matching earrings and necklace. Anwen hardly noticed, being deep in thought.

Only high-ranking guests would be in the great hall. She was sure that would include Geraint. Everyone else would eat in the other dining chambers and outside around bonfires, depending on their status. It was a relief that she wouldn't have to eat with the uncouth men Father had been entertaining before he left, but it turned her stomach knowing her people were celebrating the destruction of innocents. And her stomach twisted further when she thought about seeing Geraint again. What manner of man would she find? Captain

Arten had said he wasn't the man she'd seen ride out with revenge in his heart. But he also wasn't the carefree man she'd seen ride out with Edson all those weeks ago.

Well, tonight Anwen would do her very best to find out what manner of man he'd become. Didn't Dante say that he would need her strength and friendship? If he did, then she'd not turn her back on him. She hoped she could reconcile her conflicted emotions.

Beitris made a few minor adjustments to the accessories and smoothed out the dress one last time. She stood back to admire her work. "There. You look absolutely stunning."

Anwen blinked, registering that a response was needed. She walked over to the long looking glass mounted on the wall and studied her reflection. The excited young lady in the dress from last autumn was a woman now. Anwen turned to see tears shimmering in her maid's eyes.

"Look at you, all grown up and so beautiful."

Anwen smiled a genuine smile for the first time in weeks. "Thank you, Beitris." She took both of the maid's hands and squeezed them lightly. "Thank you for always trying to make the most of every situation. You're a good friend."

Just then, Mother returned to escort Anwen down to the great hall. But unlike Anwen, Mother still wore black, including her black veil.

Feeling apprehensive, Anwen asked in a tight and nervous voice, "How come you didn't change?"

Mother's mouth drew into a thin line, and she avoided looking at Anwen. "I knew you wouldn't be happy, so I didn't tell you."

Anwen's eyes grew wide. "Tell me what?"

Her mother held her breath and let it out slowly. "Your father said it was fine if I wore my mourning clothes but that you were to get dressed as if tonight was a party." Mother turned to walk down the passage. "Now come."

As they began to meet other people on their way to the hall, Anwen noticed that among those in mourning, like Mother, wearing black and grey, there were also a few splashes of color. Vibrant dresses worn by other young girls stood out like jewels scattered on a tabletop. Her apprehension became a hard lump of suspicion in her gut.

Grabbing her mother's arm to stop her in her tracks, Anwen asked, "I don't understand, Mother. What is this all about? Why are some of us dressed in festival clothes?"

Mother scowled down at her hand and replied in a brusque manner. "You will find out soon enough."

"So you know, and you're not telling me?" Anwen's voice rose in pitch.

"My dear, enough with these questions. Your father, *the king*, has commanded that you dress as he wishes. I do not suggest you protest." She shook off Anwen's hand and motioned for her to follow.

Typical. Mother was often an active collaborator in Father's plans. It was one of the reasons why Anwen usually didn't feel sorry for her despite the treatment she'd been suffering at Father's hands.

As they entered the great hall, Anwen saw the mead and wine were already flowing. Everyone was talking and laughing so loudly that she didn't know how anyone could hear anyone over the noise. The smells of cooked meats in rich gravies and stewed fruits mingled with people's perfumes were also overwhelming. Father looked as if he was already deep into his cups at the head of the royal table.

Was that Geraint sitting near Father? When he'd returned without her brother from Karpydosa, he'd no longer been welcome to sit at the head table. She'd hurt for him, feeling his humiliation, but she'd understood proper court etiquette. Geraint had only been part of the royal family because of Edson. Otherwise, seating at Father's table was for people of the highest rank or special guests. Young nobles of a lesser house like Geraint would rarely be accorded such an honor. She wondered what had changed.

As they approached, Geraint stood and bowed for Mother and then Anwen. His tall frame suited the style of the long-sleeved tunic. It was sage-green, which brought out the green in his eyes. His shiny blonde hair curled at his ears at the front and went to his shoulders at the back. He also had a neatly trimmed mustache and beard. Down the front of his tunic was a row of silver buttons from the collar to the hem, between two silver and black brocade panels. Around his waist, he wore a studded leather belt with a heavy silver buckle shaped like a dragon. Anwen didn't think she'd ever seen this outfit before. He certainly looked distinguished.

Before Anwen and Lethe could sit down, Father stood, raised a silver cup, and, in a booming voice, welcomed his wife and daughter. People who took notice gave a cheer.

What was going on? They hadn't done anything she knew of to be honored in such a manner. Her mother leaned toward her ear and said just loud enough to be heard, "Smile, dear. Everyone wants to see you happy."

"But why?" No one cared if she was happy. And truth be told, she wasn't happy at all. She was suspicious and nervous and did *not* want to be there.

Mother squeezed her arm so hard that Anwen was sure there would be finger-shaped bruises in the morning. Speaking through a tense smile, Mother said again, somewhat louder, "Smile."

Father's reddened eyes were on her, so Anwen smiled. She often smiled when she didn't feel like it, so today was no different. Once Father seemed satisfied and turned his attention to something else, they took their seats, and Anwen stopped smiling.

Geraint was seated two people down from her, and she could see him very well. He looked just as uncomfortable as she felt. He was fidgeting and kept glancing her way, then at her father, and back at her again. What was he trying to say? Was he trying to warn her about something? Was he trying to say anything at all? She wondered if it had something to do with their work to save the children. That thought chilled her. With Father's current state of mind, he might find it amusing to see her imprisoned in her finest dress. She felt cold sweat prickle on the back of her neck and was frustrated at not being able to talk with her co-conspirators in private, especially Geraint. It would help if she knew exactly what he was trying to communicate!

While food, wine, mead, and conversations flowed freely around her, Anwen nibbled at her food, sipped her wine, and said little. How could people celebrate something as wretched as spilling innocent blood? She would not and could not ignore her conscience. It wasn't a victory. It was a travesty, and it sickened her. If she were ever in a position of authority in need of advisors, she would remember this day and never invite those celebrating with abandon into her inner circle.

As Anwen watched her father from the corner of her eye, she felt repulsed. Gone was her innocent childhood when she had looked at him with stars in her eyes. There was a cruel light behind his eyes that were now constantly reddened by wine and lack of sleep. She noted that his hair was greyer than ever and lacked its old shine. Father had always been distant and self-absorbed, sometimes even cold and harsh, but lately, he wasn't the man she'd known all her life. Ever since Geraint's return, he seemed almost possessed by something evil.

Shakily raising her wine to her lips, Anwen hid her sickened expression behind the rim of her glass. She smoothed out her face before carefully setting the glass down and dabbing at her mouth with an embroidered linen napkin.

What was this important announcement, anyway? She wished they'd just get it over and done with. She hated every minute she had to play the happy daughter at this horrible feast. She felt completely overdone in her best gown and jewels and seeing only a few young girls similarly dressed made her feel terribly conspicuous. And Geraint, although he was also looking well-turned-out, still looked drawn and definitely uncomfortable. Somehow, she'd have to find out why.

Her father finally stood somewhat unsteadily and raised his glass once again. The noise in the room reduced to an energetic hum as heads turned toward the king. His voice boomed over the crowd as he began to speak. "Welcome, welcome! Tonight we have much to celebrate. First and most of all, we have vanquished our enemies!"

People clapped, cheered, and pounded on the tables. Anwen couldn't help herself from shrinking back against the back of her chair. Father gulped more wine before slamming his cup down on the table and laughing.

Once the raucous cheering had died down, Father continued, "Let me take this moment to honor some of my best men by name. To 'Bull Mastiff' Balcom! The best general a king could have." Father grabbed the cup that a server had hastily refilled and raised it as Balcom stood. All the men in the hall raised their cups in unison and gave a loud cheer. He bowed to the king and sat down as quickly as possible.

It went on in a similar way as Father named men who led regiments and acknowledged those still on their way back. He especially gave honor to Captain Arten and even Lord Geraint. When Geraint stood, he didn't act all puffed and proud like some. Instead, Geraint presented a serious and humble mien by bending his head at an angle, his smile subdued. She wondered if he regretted his part in her father's revenge. She hoped he did because no matter how hard she'd tried not to, she still had fluttery feelings for him.

Just as Anwen thought her father would be winding down his speech, he surprised her with another announcement. "And, what better time to have a second celebration! After the feasting, there will be a ball. All our young ladies, please stand."

All the young ladies dressed in colored gowns stood. Some of them smiled or giggled, while others looked stiff and unhappy. Once again, there were cheers and shouted comments. Anwen tensed but didn't move to stand. For once, she was glad of Mother's restraining hand on her shoulder. "What's going on?"

As Father raised his cup for another toast, Mother quickly replied, "It's not your turn."

Before Anwen could ask what she meant, Father continued, "Now, I have the duty and the pleasure to announce a number of marriages that were contracted at the Midwinter festivities but delayed due to Karpydosa's betrayal. Tonight, the young ladies of our court will meet their intended husbands, some for the very first time!"

He waved his cup, pointing at the audience. "Lords and Ladies of my court, take note." He waited as people laughed and then added, "Most importantly, this night is a betrothal ceremony of great significance! You know my daughter, Princess Anwen, is now of age. Being the heir apparent, she needs a strong man by her side, one loyal to me, the king, and our beloved Kingdom of Livania. And so, tonight, I would also like to announce the betrothal of my daughter, Princess Anwen!"

Anwen felt as though she was going to faint. She'd never thought much about her eventual marriage, preferring not to think of the man she might be forced to marry. Never in a million years had she thought she'd find out like this, with *no* consideration and *no* warning. On second thought, she was more likely to vomit than faint. Anwen was sure she'd never hated anyone more than she did her father at that moment. She stared at him as she listened to the announcement that would define her future.

When the hall had quietened down to an anticipatory hum, the king's voice boomed through the room, "I present to you my daughter's betrothed, Lord Geraint of Elmsbridge, soon-to-be husband and consort to Princess Anwen!"

If Anwen thought the noise from people cheering before had been loud, it now grew to a deafening roar. People started coming forward to congratulate them, but Anwen sat completely still, stunned into silence, her hearing muffled as if she were underwater. Faces she should have recognized but didn't seem to register loomed closer. She blinked slowly at them. They spoke, but their voices were muffled and strange. Someone pulled her limp hand into theirs and squeezed while others patted her shoulders before moving away again. What was going on?

Mother pinched her hard on the inside of her wrist, the one lying limp in her lap. It hurt enough for everything to come crashing back. Anwen snatched her other hand away from the next person shaking it and jerked her head toward Geraint. He was standing, surrounded by people congratulating him. How long had he known, and why hadn't he said anything? He could have come to see her or, at least, written her a note!

Once again, she was the last to find out.

When Father's attention was elsewhere, Anwen turned to her mother. A sharp pain shot through her chest, and her voice shook as she asked over the noise, "Did you know?"

"Don't make a scene, Daughter."

So what if she was making a scene. She wasn't going to pretend that everything was alright.

Hot tears pricked her eyes, but there was no way she'd give in to tears now. Anwen clutched the napkin in her lap and asked again, "Did you?" The people who should protect her had betrayed her. Even Mother hadn't done the decent thing and let her know. So many people were watching her reactions, seeing how clueless she was. Anwen held the napkin to her face, something to hide the hurt and humiliation.

Mother leaned close and said, "This was the special announcement I mentioned earlier." Patting her arm in a supposedly reassuring way, she added, "It was my idea to make it a ball with the announcement of other betrothals so you wouldn't feel as singled out, having to carry the focus of attention."

A strangled sound escaped Anwen.

In a defensive voice, Mother said, "I couldn't say more than that. Your father wanted it to be a surprise."

Wiping the napkin angrily across her eyes and nose, she replied, "Well, I'm definitely surprised!"

Shaking her head, Mother said, "Don't be so dramatic. Geraint is young and handsome, well-loved by everyone, and he has gained the king's favor. You should be happy. You know, you could have done far worse."

"That's beside the point, Mother!"

Mother's face pinched as if she'd eaten something sour. So what if Mother was displeased with her outburst. If anyone had a reason to feel unhappy, Anwen certainly did, and if Mother's deception led her to feel guilty, so be it!

Her hands trembled as she twisted the napkin between her fingers. Anwen was heartsick, beyond angry, with Father, Mother, Geraint, and everyone else for participating in this farce. But Father was watching her now with his cold, judgmental eyes. Once again, she had to play along or face the consequences. Anwen forced a smile, but it didn't reach her eyes. Father frowned, and Mother pinched her again, even harder, causing fresh tears to gather at the corners of her eyes. She smiled through them and began acknowledging the people congratulating her. They probably thought these were happy tears. Father gave an approving nod and went back to his feasting and conversation.

As the well-wishers dispersed, returning to their seats or gathering in excited little groups, Geraint came up behind her. Anwen looked up at him, her gaze filled with anger, hurt, and disappointment. His eyes looked apologetic and uncharacteristically pleading. He took her hand to pull her to her feet. She tensed her arm, wanting to yank it back but, at the same time, not wanting to attract Father's attention. Geraint reacted by tightening his grip. He leaned down to kiss her cheek and quickly said, "Please, play along a bit longer, and then you can yell at me all you want in private."

She remained tense and angry but got to her feet, feeling the kiss like a brand on her cheek. People began cheering again for the "happy" couple. Geraint held her hand and smiled at the crowd. He leaned close to her ear, tickling her neck with his breath. "Your father is allowing us a brief time to speak together in private," he said over the noise, but only loudly enough for her to hear.

"Well, that is very kind of him!" Anwen snarled back, wishing she could snatch her hand from his grip.

That irresistible eyebrow of his popped up, and he gave her a crooked smile. This time it didn't work on her. Anwen was so angry she wanted to punch him right in the face.

Geraint raised her hand to his lips and kissed the back of it. "Do you trust me?"

Her breath hitched, and she stared at her hand in his. "I used to," she replied bitterly. Anwen glanced up and caught him wince. She knew her words had stung, but he deserved them.

As if he'd read her thoughts, he said, "I deserved that." He placed her hand on his bent forearm. "Let's go where we can talk in private for a few minutes. Shall we?"

Instead of resisting any further, Anwen nodded. She needed a quiet moment to gather her thoughts and make sense of this latest development.

Geraint led the way, holding her hand on his arm as if she might change her mind and make a run for it. As they walked out together, people cheered again. She'd had enough of all the noise and the crowd. Feeling drained, Anwen found herself leaning against his arm for support.

Once they'd left the great hall, Geraint slowly led her along the passage. "Are you alright?" he asked, his voice full of concern.

Well, his concern was too little too late! Her anger spiked, renewing her strength. "No, I'm not alright." She stopped and jerked her hand off Geraint's arm, rubbing it down her skirt as if removing something vile. She was past caring about the silk of her dress.

He allowed her to pull away, but as they approached the stairs, he placed his hand on her lower back. Anwen flinched, not welcoming his touch, but she couldn't walk faster, and his hand remained.

"Please, Anwen," Geraint said pleadingly. "We don't have much time. Soon we'll have to return and present ourselves at the ball."

His voice sounded so sorrowful that Anwen couldn't help feeling sorry for him. As she released a huge sigh, she let go of the anger and tension, allowing her shoulders to drop. When she began to feel the warmth of his large hand through her gown, she stopped caring which way they were heading. Was his hand trembling, or was she shivering at his touch? Perhaps it was both.

They reached the balcony alcove where Anwen had eventually found him after his return from Karpydosa. Was it only a few weeks ago? So much had happened this past spring, much of which she'd witnessed from this balcony.

No longer would she look at the world through the innocent eyes of a child. No longer could she trust the men who ruled without questioning their motives. She would carry the pain of King Marin's betrayal and the shame of Father's revenge for the rest of her life. And worst of all, she'd learned that Father couldn't be trusted in anything. He may have chosen the one man that Anwen loved as her future husband, but he hadn't done it for her. He'd done it for his own selfish reasons. She could just as easily be marrying some ancient moneylender.

Geraint hadn't spoken again, and she wondered what was going through his mind. Had he been secretly in love with her as she had with him? She wasn't really sure. Neither of them had been free to act on any feelings or even discuss them, so it simply hadn't mattered. But tonight, everything had changed with Father's shocking announcement. Was Geraint nervous? She certainly was. She shivered again. Was it from anger, anticipation, or the cold night air on the balcony? She wasn't sure.

It was dark outside, the only light coming from the moon, stars, and distant bonfires in the courtyard. The lively music of flutes, harps, and tambourines drifted up to them as people danced and were generally having a good time.

As her eyes adjusted in the dim light, she noticed blankets resting on the seat ledge. "Did you put those here?" Anwen asked, surprised.

"Yes, I knew we would need a place to talk." Geraint sounded hesitant and apologetic. "This seemed like the logical place." He turned to face her, placing his hands on her upper arms.

Standing in the shelter of the balcony and shrouded by darkness, Anwen had no fear that anyone below would see them. Her arms felt hot wherever Geraint touched her, and she forgot about the cold night air. It was just him and her. The world and all her troubles fell away as she focused on his voice.

"I told your father that you wouldn't like being surprised about something like this, but he insisted I keep silent. I feel terrible for not having had this conversation ahead of time, and tonight you looked so beautiful..." He brushed a stray strand of hair away from her face. "I hated to see how being blindsided by this announcement made you feel. But that's the reason why I've been avoiding you. I didn't trust myself not to tell you, and no one was allowed to. If you hadn't seemed genuinely surprised, heads would have rolled. Maybe not literally, but the punishment would have been unpleasant, and with the way your father has been behaving, heads may have actually rolled."

Anwen couldn't see his face clearly, but she could hear the sincere desperation in his voice. Everything Geraint said made sense, but the words and the apology were still hard to accept. Father had made a fool of her in front of everyone. She *knew* they could see she had no idea about what was going on. Well, she was tired of Father's games. He had a way of crushing a person's spirit, but she wasn't going to play anymore. She shivered. Defying Father could have some serious repercussions.

Geraint grabbed a blanket. "Allow me." He wrapped it around her shoulders while leading her back to the seat ledge and adjusting the blankets for her to sit. "I know you must have a thousand questions, and I'll do my best to answer them. Well, the ones I'm able to answer anyway." He wrapped another blanket snuggly around her legs before doing the same for himself. They both leaned comfortably back against the wall.

Anwen let out a tired sigh. Most of the fight and anger were gone now, leaving a numbness behind. "So, how long have you known?"

"If it makes you feel any better, I've only known for a few days." Geraint tipped his head, looking out at the starry sky.

Taking Anwen's cold hands in his, he rubbed them until they grew warm. "After everything that's happened, I know I don't deserve you. And if you don't want to marry me, I completely understand, no matter the reason. I'll tell your father, and I'll take the blame. If there is someone else, I'll do my best to sway him for your sake." He cleared his throat. "Is there someone else?"

There wasn't anyone else, and Anwen shook her head no, forgetting he couldn't see her clearly.

"Was that a no or yes?" he asked.

"No, there's no one," she said breathily. Anwen could feel her face heating with embarrassment. At least in the dark, he couldn't read the telltale signs of a girl who'd loved him secretly for so long. But was she ready to tell him, to trust him with her heart?

Letting out a shaky laugh, Geraint continued, "For many years, I've thought that having you as my wife could only ever be a dream and never a reality. Now I have my dream, but I feel the circumstances are terrible and that maybe you think I'm an awful choice for a husband." He squeezed her hands. "Please, say something."

"I'm... I don't know what to say."

It made sense that Geraint had been the one chosen for her, having studied and trained alongside Edson all those years. Father knew how close the two had been and how loyal Geraint had been. He knew Geraint and his abilities well. Father probably thought he would be easy to control and always loyal to him, especially if he used a royal marriage as a bribe. Anwen was bitter that none of her feelings had been taken into consideration. But the joke was on her father in the end. She loved Geraint, and Father couldn't have picked a more suitable husband as far as she was concerned!

Anwen opened her mouth, her confession of love on the tip of her tongue, but Geraint jumped in before she could form the words. "It was the good captain who advised me not to decline your father's offer. I wanted to, you know. Decline. For your sake." He shifted her hands into one of his, rubbing his face with the other. "I'm sorry. Trying to put things into words is so hard."

"It's... It's alright. I think I understand," Anwen said quietly.

"Well, I need to say this so that I'm sure you really understand." Geraint looked out over the courtyard and then back at her. "Arten told me if I didn't accept, someone else would, someone who might not know you as I do. Someone who might not care about you." He touched her cheek with his free hand. "Someone who would see you only as a stepping stone to the crown, not as someone to love."

She'd thought she understood but now wasn't so sure. "So, you thought you wanted me but then decided that you didn't? You only agreed to marry me out of pity?"

"What? No!" He grabbed her face between his warm, calloused hands and leaned close, their noses almost touching. "I never stopped wanting you. But I thought you could do better than me." He rested his forehead briefly against hers as if caving in on himself. But then he quickly straightened and added cheekily, "And besides, another man might not allow you to meddle."

Anwen huffed out a laugh. "Are you saying you will allow me to meddle?"

"Yes. That's what I'm saying." His voice became warm and sincere as he added, "And you have the captain's approval, among others."

Something burst free inside her, and tears began sliding down her cheeks.

"I remember you recently asking me for help," Geraint spoke softly, his voice thick with emotion. "And, I want to always be the one to help you." He wiped her tears with his thumbs and continued, this time a little louder, "As your humble servant, I promise you my fealty. As your humble husband, I promise you my love."

He took both her hands and raised them to his lips, kissing the knuckle of each finger.

Encouraged by his kisses and words, Anwen replied, "Geraint, I have only ever had eyes for you. There has never been another, and I never thought I'd get the chance to be with you."

Geraint leaned in and nuzzled her cheek down to her neck. His short beard scraped lightly against her skin. Resting his forehead against her shoulder, he breathed her in. After several breaths that tickled her neck, he leaned back again and released her hands. Bereft of his touch, she felt cold. She wanted the contact, *needed* it even, and was about to lean in, to close the distance, when he said, "But I'm not the same man I was before all this happened. I might not be what you want anymore." His voice grew thin and strained, "I'm not even what I want me to be anymore."

This time Anwen took his hands in hers. "Yes, you lost your way for a time. But that does not define you as a person. I've known you almost my whole life, and you are a good man." She gently squeezed his hands before letting go. "None of us are perfect. We all make mistakes. What's important is that you acknowledge your mistakes and do the best you can as you go forward from here." Encouraged by the word of Riaas to be strong for him, Anwen added, "I will be by your side if you will be by mine."

Geraint exhaled loudly. Gently tilting Anwen's chin up, he once again leaned in close, his lips almost touching hers. "I don't deserve you. But I do love you." He pressed his smooth lips against hers and kissed her. First softly and then more firmly, his whiskers prickling her sensitive skin. The sensation was new but not unpleasant.

Anwen parted her lips on a sigh, and Geraint "mmmed" softly in return. She sighed again, and he chuckled a little. Anwen smiled as Geraint peppered her with little kisses on her lips and beside her mouth. His short beard tickled, and she made a soft sound of complaint mixed with surprised delight.

His calloused hands held her face gently, and he said in a teasing tone, "You're supposed to kiss back."

Anwen giggled, feeling lighthearted for the first time in what felt like centuries. "It's my first time being kissed," she offered by way of explanation. It was a heady experience, and she was determined to enjoy every moment.

A low laugh rumbled from Geraint, and he kissed her with more fervor. This time she was ready for it and kissed him back. When his tongue found hers, she moved slightly away in surprise, but he stroked the back of her neck and shoulders, encouraging her to come closer. Once she accepted this new sensation, she enjoyed exploring his lips and tongue with her own. He deepened the kiss, and she wondered if she would have enough room to breathe. But soon, he softened the pressure and slowly pulled his lips away from hers.

Sighing happily, Anwen leaned her head against his shoulder. Geraint shifted, momentarily moving her away. She was about to protest, but he opened his blanket and tucked her in against his side. Anwen sighed again, enjoying the warmth, and he chuckled.

"So, Princess. If your father has his way, we will be married as soon as the proper period for mourning is over, before the winter sets in. How do you feel about that?" When she didn't reply, he hastily added, "Or I could try to convince him to postpone until next spring."

"But why?" Anwen asked, her voice muffled by the blanket. "I'm happy to marry before winter."

"Really? Well, if you're happy, then I'm also happy." He squeezed her and kissed the top of her head.

Lifting her face away from the blanket, Anwen asked, "Have you thought about our future and that we will one day rule Livania? Father won't live forever, not if he keeps abusing his health as he has been." She didn't tell Geraint about the words she'd received from Riaas. There would be time later to discuss them, if she chose to do so.

Geraint held Anwan by the shoulders as he looked her in the eyes. "I think I understand the question. But what is it you really want to know?"

Placing her hand against Geraint's steadily beating heart, Anwen replied, "Father can't control me forever. Once he is gone... Well, one day, possibly sooner rather than later, I'll become the queen of Livania, and you will be my royal consort. It's not something I previously expected or trained for. Edson was to be king, and I was to cement an alliance with an arranged marriage. I was content with that, but now..." Her voice trailed off, but then she quickly added, "How do you feel about that?"

Geraint smiled, his teeth flashing white against the moonlight. "Say that again."

"Say what again?"

"I'll be your..." he paused, waiting for something.

"Oh." Her eyes grew wide. "Do you mean 'my royal consort'?"

"Yes, that." Geraint pressed her hand more firmly against his heart. "I love the sound of it."

Anwen giggled and poked him playfully. "I'm being serious here, my supposedly humble husband-to-be. How do you feel about me outranking you?"

Geraint let his blanket drop as he shifted to cup her face. "My darling princess, I am not concerned about your rank. I have already said I will be your humble servant *and* your humble husband." Reaching for her hands again, he continued, "Concerning your father, we will very carefully do our best. You have won the respect of Captain Arten and even of Commander Balcom. You have all our support. We stand by you now and one day as our queen."

Anwen looked down at their joined hands and then up into his eyes. It sounded too good to be true, yet somehow, she believed him. "That's... That's perfect." Her heart felt full to bursting. "I... I don't know what else to say."

"Tell me you love me," he said, his voice growing husky.

She dipped her head and said shyly, "I love you."

"And I love you." Geraint cupped her face again with his hand and growled, "Just one more kiss before we have to return."

Anwen barely got in an "mm-hmm" before his lips were on hers. This kiss was nothing like the previous kisses. It was desperate and full of emotion, giving her a taste of the depths of his love.

All too soon, Geraint pulled his lips away and sighed. "We'd best return to the hall." He stood, holding out his hands. "We've been too long already."

Anwen set the blankets aside and took Geraint's hands. "Let's go," she said.

The two of them made their way to the hall. This time, Anwen was ready and determined. They could face any future, as long as they did it together.

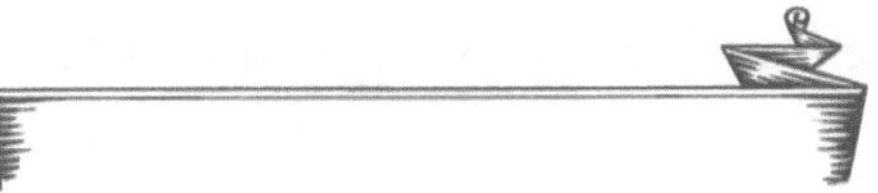

Chapter 17
Sacrificial Servant

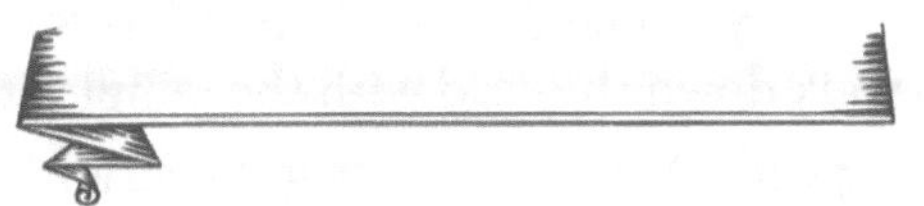

PAXTON DIDN'T UNDERSTAND any of his feelings when it came to Amity. He either really liked and admired her or was angry with her for being so happy all the time, depending on his mood. She didn't act like any of the other girls he knew. She seemed happy helping with the little kids instead of hanging out with the other girls her age, gossiping, rearranging her hair, and looking at the boys. He didn't understand her at all.

Amity wasn't beautiful, not one bit, but she had a unique quality about her. She was tall for her age with carved features that somehow looked "pure" or something. But thinking of her in that way seemed way too solemn. Her thick ash-brown hair looked amazing when she wore it loose with only the sides tied up. He didn't want Amity or anyone else to know that he liked her hair. That would be the last thing he needed! Calling her "Ashes" was a spur-of-the-moment thing, but it allowed him to talk about her without anyone being the wiser. And the few times he got close enough to see her grey eyes, they mesmerized him. Framed by long black lashes, they were like a cloudy sky.

The fifteen and sixteen-year-old girls who hung around him and his friends liked talking about silly things, but whenever he overheard Amity, she was caring and thoughtful, explaining things to the little kids so they could understand. And, could that girl sing! Amity had a clear, strong voice that made you want to stop what you were doing and just listen.

But then there was all that rot and snot about Fate and Destiny. Paxton had been learning that stuff way longer than Amity. What did she know? His grandparents had had the brightest of destinies, and he'd always aspired to be like them. And, now? He felt tricked. He felt cheated. Riaas had let them all down. What purpose was there in having a "destiny" or following Riaas if he was just going to sit back and allow injustice to prevail?

Oddly, since they'd been on the road, Paxton had noticed an uncomfortable feeling between his shoulder blades, pushing through his chest. It wasn't the kind of pain you get from being punched, but one that kind of burned, and it was always there, making him feel unhappy and uncooperative. He hadn't felt normal since hugging his grandparents, saying his last goodbye, and then turning to walk down the road with the temple at his back.

That was the thing with Amity. She thought everything was sunshine and roses, and that drove Paxton mad. He'd never seen anyone smile so much! He liked that about her and hated it at the same time. Didn't Amity care that people were dying? Didn't she see how unfair everything was? How could she keep acting as if nothing was going wrong? Sometimes he couldn't stand it!

The first time Paxton didn't see her smiling, he called her out on it. It was one particularly windy, wretched, cold spring day full of intermittent showers. They were all trudging along, except for the children bundled into wagons. Amity was walking alone, looking miserable like everyone else. "Hey! Ashes! You're not smiling. I thought you always smile!"

Amity had stopped walking and looked his way. "Who says I'm always smiling?"

Goading her was kind of fun, especially when she got those sparks in her eyes as she did on this occasion. Wanting to irritate her further, Paxton had thumbed his chest and replied, "I do. I see you with a big grin on your face every day. So what do you have to say about that?" He smirked as he awaited her reply.

The sparks in her eyes had died, and she looked down. Without giving him a reply, Amity had simply turned and continued walking. And she didn't look back.

Even though it happened three days ago, Paxton could remember that moment clearly. He had felt a little ashamed. And now? Now he found that he was sort of missing her quiet grey regard. Well, that was great. More feelings to add to his unrest and disagreeability. Paxton kicked a stone hard enough to bounce it off one of the trees beside the path, bruising his first two toes. He muttered a few words he was not supposed to know and continued walking.

Up ahead, Amity was walking by herself. Paxton was often looking her way, only realizing it when he did. Summer was near, and most people were in good spirits, but he couldn't say the same for her. She had been alone all day and hadn't spent any of it smiling. After his comments the other day and considering how the other novices were treating her, he was pretty sure she wouldn't be smiling any time soon, either. He felt a little guilty about that.

Sure, Paxton gave Amity a hard time, but she wasn't the type of girl to make things easy for him either. In fact, she was the only girl their age that he knew who didn't. But, just maybe, he liked her that way. The other girls were agreeable all the time. They giggled or complimented anything he did. They made it obvious they wanted his attention. They played coy, batted their lashes, and knew all the tricks, but Amity was different. Paxton realized, a little alarmingly, that he found her more intriguing than any of the other girls.

What did the fellow in that book he had been reading say? Oh right, he "was drawn to her like a fruit fly to red wine. And, unlike that hapless fruit fly, he hoped not to drown in her sweet, sweet wine." Okay, maybe it wasn't great literature, but it made him feel insightful and, just maybe, a little worldly. But, oh boy, he better not get caught reading that kind of stuff by his mother. She would have him peeling potatoes forever if she *ever* found out. She was a real stickler about what she said was "suitable reading for young men."

Mother came from a family of wealthy merchants who were "very aware" of their social position in the City of Tilmar. Paxton never understood how his grandparents had come to name their daughter Prudence, it didn't seem like the kind of name they'd like, but it seemed to fit her perfectly. He also sometimes wondered how she'd come to be an ordained of Riaas. It didn't seem like a *logical* thing to happen when all his aunts ever seemed to talk about were his cousins making advantageous marriages, buying new gowns, or going to parties. Also, no one on that side of the family seemed to be at all religious, although they did celebrate Midsummer and Midwinter the same as everyone else.

Everyone on Mother's side of the family had always adored him, but Paxton was never comfortable in his grandparents' huge house. Whenever she had taken him for a visit, he would always have to wear his best clothes and be on his best behavior. He also felt really strange being waited on by servants and missed the constant bustle of the monastery. He would try to avoid going as often as possible, and, a few times, managed to convince Mother to leave him behind, but she was so persistent, saying how much everyone looked forward to seeing him. Father had often made excuses and could usually claim to have "pressing work" to get out of going with them. He had empathized with Father even if he wasn't sure about his reasons, but he suspected that Father's reasons were the same as his own.

Strange, Paxton never thought he would ever miss those visits to his grandparents, but now he did, and thinking about the goodbye letter he had written to them made him angry at the king, at Riaas, and this whole stupid mess all over again! He'd been mad at Mother too. She'd made him rewrite that letter twice! At least she'd only required that he write one letter for the entire family. She'd told him that his first attempts had been too impersonal and that he should dig deep and connect with his feelings. But all he'd been feeling was numb and angry. Now he was glad she'd made him do it, even if writing that bit of "heartfelt" nonsense had felt like a lie at the time.

He still didn't always understand his feelings, especially when they got all jumbled up, leaving him in bewildered knots. But did he really want Amity to be as miserable as he was? Well, no, probably not. And why did his thoughts keep circling back to her anyway? She hardly ever spoke to him and didn't even seem to like him. He figured that giving her a hard time was a good excuse to talk to her. Mostly he was just teasing her rather than being mean. Several of the other novices *were* mean, and things had started getting out of hand, especially lately.

Since the incident with the cabbages, the other girls were deliberately trying to make her look clumsy and accident-prone. The latest thing had happened just last night. After they were finished setting up camp, the canvas that Amity had been sitting under "inexplicably" collapsed right on top of her, making her look ridiculous as she crawled out from under it. She wasn't hurt, so Paxton didn't say anything, but he knew it wasn't an accident. The girls had laughed and made a lot of jokes at her expense, and they'd pulled the boys in on it too. During supper, she'd been very quiet and hadn't eaten much. Now they had a new name for her, "Amity Calamity."

The teasing and mean-spirited comments had gotten so bad today that even the young children had stopped walking with her. It wasn't long before Amity was left all on her own, walking between the different clusters of people. Part of him felt bad and wanted it all to stop, but another part of him felt kind of good about it in a small nasty way, and he hoped that it would finally shake her steadfast faith in Riaas. Right now, he felt completely betrayed by their god. He didn't understand how anyone could still believe in him, not after everything that had transpired.

Traveling through the Kingdom of Bariny had taken their group nearly five weeks pushing hard with almost four hundred people of all ages, horses and wagons, a small flock of goats, and a dozen milk cows. They'd slowed their pace upon entering the mountain pass five days ago as it was harder going. The road led up and through the Whistling Mountains and down into the Kingdom of Tandola. They would then pass through the Kingdom of Corithane and eventually arrive in the Kingdom of Penthia.

Messages carried by lightweight riders on fast horses and then by ship across the South Sea had already been sent to the Temple of Riaas in Penthia explaining their plight. What would he do once they got there? Paxton didn't know, as he didn't want to serve Riaas anymore. He didn't want to think about it either. Well, he'd have to wait and see.

As the road began to wind upward, it grew steeper and narrower with rocky terrain, piles of boulders, and increasingly sharper slopes on either side. Everyone had to walk in smaller groups that were strung out along the trail. Paxton's group had shrunk to only male novices his age and younger. Many of them were friends, but several of the younger boys were new, and Paxton didn't know them well. They were bored with walking, and Amity seemed to be the main topic of entertainment that afternoon.

A new boy named Hileon said he wanted to see what would happen if he pushed "Amity Calamity" into the stinging nettles growing abundantly alongside the road. Paxton didn't like Hileon and thought he was the sort of boy who would do just about anything for attention, but he didn't voice an opinion, one way or another. Some of the others goaded Hileon on, though he didn't need much encouragement. Soon, Hileon was carefully jogging up behind Amity. He slowed as he quietly walked closer, staying directly behind her. At the right moment, when none of the adults were close enough to see, he pushed her hard, between the shoulder blades. Paxton winced as Amity went off the road, using her outstretched hands to break the fall. At least she didn't land with her face into the horrible plants or against the rocky ground.

"Hey, look at Amity Calamity!" yelled Hileon, pointing out Amity's latest "accident."

Jumping back up, Amity looked anxiously at her scraped palms. Paxton knew how horrible stinging nettle rash could be. It had a nasty way of itching and burning, but only a little at first, raising small blisters and, within minutes, becoming really painful. She wouldn't feel it immediately, but it wouldn't be long before she did.

Feeling bad for Amity and guilty because he had allowed Hileon to hurt her, Paxton quickly grabbed for his canteen. Hastening toward her, he pulled the stopper, ready to help flush away the nettle juice. By the time he reached Amity, tears were silently streaming down her face as she dabbed her scraped and burning palms on her dress.

While they stood by the side of the road, Paxton took ahold of one of her hands, poured water over it, and then gently wiped at her palm with a clean handkerchief. She tried yanking her hand away a few times, but he ignored her attempts.

She finally raised her voice at him and said, "Just leave me alone! Let me go!"

Looking into her humiliated, tear-filled eyes, he said in frustration, "I'm only trying to help you!"

"You're part of the problem. In fact, you're the one who started all of this. So, I don't *want* or *need* your help!"

Standing at his full height with eyes narrowed, Paxton exclaimed, "What do you mean, I started it?"

Just then they heard Amity's name being called. They both turned to see one of the ordained couples hurrying up the road to them. Priest Justin was a tall thin man with a lean no-nonsense face. Priestess Grace had rosy cheeks and motherly curves. She was carrying a healer's kit in a canvas bag over her shoulder and wore a concerned frown.

Paxton began to feel a little nervous as they drew near. He suspected that they would be inclined to take Amity's side if they thought there was some kind of dispute. They knew her well and liked her very much, as they had young children she looked after regularly.

As they stood at the side of the road together, Justin asked, "What's going on here?"

"I tripped and fell off the trail into stinging nettles, Sir," Amity said quietly through her tears.

Paxton was surprised by Amity's answer. Hileon deserved to be reported. Why wouldn't she take the opportunity to get back at him?

Justin was a man who didn't miss much, and he didn't seem at all convinced. Looking at Paxton's face and Amity's hands, he asked sharply, "You tripped and fell, or you were pushed?"

Priestess Grace was already sorting through her healer kit, pulling out a cloth, a few strips of bandages, and a small tub of mouse ear salve. She "tsked" as she attended to Amity's hands. "These are going to be tender," she told her. "You aren't to be washing dishes or doing anything to irritate them for a few days."

Justin gave Paxton a sharp look, and Paxton cringed a little. He knew from experience not much got past the priest. "Amity didn't want to get me into trouble, but it was me, Sir. We had a little quarrel. I kind of lost my temper, and it just happened. I'm sorry, and I promise not to do it again." Did he just say that? What had come over him to be the sacrificial servant?

People were maneuvering around them on the narrow road, so they pushed further to the edge.

"I'm very disappointed in you, Paxton. You should know better. You're no longer a child. You're a young man and must govern yourself as an adult. You could have caused Amity to suffer a serious injury! You know we could lose valuable time if someone got hurt badly enough, and we had to stop moving." Priest Justin gave Paxton a stern and disappointed look.

Paxton winced and rubbed a hand along the back of his neck. He could feel the color blazing from his cheeks.

Priest Justin continued, "Maybe you and your friends are only trying to amuse yourselves, or you're just not thinking about the consequences, but you must never hurt others with your actions. I'm sure you're aware that the others look up to you, and you need to lead by example."

Paxton's face fell. He hadn't thought he could feel any worse or so small. Priest Justin was right, of course, and Paxton didn't have any excuse. He just hadn't thought about it, having never suffered from anything other than the good-natured teasing and ragging that boys regularly indulged in. "Yes, Sir. I'm truly sorry. I promise to do better."

"And, you will. Starting now. Amity could use your assistance."

Paxton glanced her way, but Amity refused to make eye contact.

The priest continued, "She has been a blessing to those of us with children, keeping them entertained at the temple and during this long and difficult journey. She could use some help devising games to keep the children busy as we go along, especially now that she is injured."

Paxton scrunched up his face, feeling very unhappy with the idea of herding a flock of small children over a mountain pass.

Before he could open his mouth to say so, Justin spoke again, "Or, would you rather I discussed this incident with your parents?"

Paxton grimaced and reluctantly said, "No, Sir."

"Have I made myself clear?"

Shuffling his feet, Paxton replied, "Yes, Sir."

"Now, apologize to Amity."

He couldn't read Amity's face, but her eyes were intense. He flinched, feeling remorseful. "I'm sorry."

Eyes still shimmering with tears, Amity nodded.

Priest Justin "hmmed" in his throat, then looked sharply at Paxton. "I hope you will remember what I've said. We still have a long way to travel, and we all need to help one another so we can reach our destination safely." He turned to his wife and held out his hand.

Priestess Grace smiled and took the proffered hand. Turning again to Amity, she said, "Come and find me later to change those bandages. I'll give you some supplies to look after those scrapes, but don't hesitate if you want me to look at them at any time."

The couple stepped away and continued walking up the road hand in hand.

Only after they began walking away did Amity's expression turn stormy and she hissed, "You should be sorry! Like I said before, you started with the name-calling. Things only got worse after that."

Paxton was surprised at the sudden change in her, so surprised that he didn't take time to think through his response. "It's not what you think. When I started calling you Ashes, it was meant as a nickname because of that ashy silver-brown color in your hair."

Amity's mouth dropped open. When she spoke, her tone was both incredulous and reproachful. "What? Are you crazy? What makes you think that *Ashes* is a good nickname? Because I'll tell you that none of the others saw it that way. Did you ever try setting them straight?"

"Umm, not exactly."

She stared, her grey eyes glinting like granite. "And why not?"

"Because..."

"Because... Why?"

Paxton didn't want to tell her why, but she was, obviously, not going to let this go. Dropping his voice, he said, "I didn't want anyone knowing that I like your hair."

Amity's eyebrows rose to her hairline and then drew down again. "You *like* it?" She looked furious.

Paxton looked down at his feet. His confession embarrassed him, and her anger made him uncomfortable.

"So, you're a coward *and* a bully." She huffed.

Paxton looked up, blurting out the first thing that came to mind, "Aren't all bullies cowards?" Immediately, he wished he'd said nothing, even if Paxton didn't think he fit in the bullies and cowards category. Well, too late for that.

"I guess it would take one to know one!"

"Look, I'm trying to apologize here. Don't make it any harder."

"Well, you deserve it," Amity bit out. "And I don't care if it's hard for you!"

Paxton wished she would keep it down. He didn't want anyone reporting this conversation to his mother. His body vibrated with anger and embarrassment, and he spoke in a low, harsh tone, "I deserve it? Look at you all high and mighty. If anyone deserves to be poked at a little, it's you!"

"Why? What did I ever do to you?" Flinging out her bandaged hands, she added, "I've hardly even spoken to you before today, and only because you spoke to me first, Mr. Perfect!"

"Because you're always so happy. You act like nothing is wrong. All. The. Time."

Suddenly, as if from out of nowhere, Priest Justin appeared. "Paxton! What did I tell you?"

"Sorry, Sir." Though still angry and embarrassed, Paxton managed to keep his tone level as he addressed the priest. Where had the man *come* from?!

In the meantime, his friends had caught up to them. They had witnessed the last part of the exchange, but they sure didn't want to get involved. They gave Paxton a few sympathetic looks before they hurried past with their heads down. Well, fine. So, they felt sorry for him. Well, he felt sorry for himself too!

And he hadn't even pushed her! Where was Hileon anyway? He was going to make that sorry little fink pay for this.

Turning on her heel with her nose in the air, Amity marched up the trail. Paxton quickly caught up to her, but she completely ignored him. How could he help her if she was going to act like this? What was the point?

Annoyed, he clenched his hands. But as he did so, Paxton noticed how Amity held hers, being careful not to even brush them against her dress. Suddenly, he felt deflated. Paxton might not have actually pushed her into the stinging nettles, but he had, in a way, had a role in Hileon injuring her today. Also, he'd been the one who had started the name-calling and hadn't bothered to defend her when others had taken it further than he'd ever meant it to go. It had made her vulnerable to a series of escalating pranks. He'd gotten the ball rolling, and then he'd lost control. He'd pretended not to see the damage it was doing as it rolled downhill, gaining in size and speed. He realized that he was, at least, partly to blame, if not mostly. *Rot and snot!*

Finally looking over at Paxton, Amity let out a huge breath. "I'm not always happy! I get sad and scared just like everyone else." Her voice vibrated with frustration.

Oh, so she was still stuck on that comment of his. Wonderful.

She continued, her voice rising a little, "I just don't let it take over my life. You could do the same, so stop resenting me for that! Stop taking your problems out on me!" She sucked in a breath and sniffed.

Maybe *Amity* thought she'd said enough, but Paxton wasn't ready to let her have the last word. "Prove it!" he demanded. "When were you sad or scared but smiling anyway?"

"Do you really want to know, or do you just want to keep making up your own dumb ideas about me?" She tossed her head in the air while stomping up the road.

Had he been making up his own ideas about her? Dumb ones? Taking a deep breath, Paxton relented. "I suppose maybe I have been. So...?"

Those grey eyes looked suspiciously back at him. "So... What?"

"So, tell me. I want to know."

No one was within earshot, but Amity still looked around and lowered her voice. "I never thought I'd have to give up everything and flee my homeland when I became a novice at the temple. It was so hard not being able to say goodbye to my family. They'll be so worried when they hear about what's happened." Her voice hitched as she added, "It'll be a long time before I find out if they even got my letter. I plan to write once we get to Penthia, and, hopefully, I'll hear back. But that will take months!"

Another tear ran down her cheek, and Amity quickly swiped it away with the back of one hand and continued. "My eldest sister is getting married this summer. I really wanted to be there for Esme's wedding. And two precious gifts I had from my mama and papa are missing. And... Well, I'm never going to see them again." After taking a shaky breath, she added, "I'm n-never going to see any of my family ever again." There was a quiver in her voice, and fresh tears fell from Amity's eyes.

Oh, wow. Paxton hadn't considered that. Leaving his loved ones behind had been hard, but he still had his parents and good friends like Henry. He hadn't really thought about what anyone else was leaving behind. But there was something else she'd said that niggled at him. Maybe there was something he could do to help. "What do you mean your things are missing? Were they lost?"

Amity wiped her eyes on her sleeve before replying, "No, n-not lost."

Paxton could tell by her expression that she didn't believe, one bit, that her things were lost.

Building on his suspicion, she added, "They are *missing*."

"What? No one from the temple would just take them!"

When Amity didn't respond, Paxton tried again, "You should be able to trust everyone here. No one should be stealing!"

"Hmmph." She shook her head.

"Look, maybe I can help, if you tell me." Frustrated at her silence, Paxton added more forcefully, "Tell me!"

Amity glanced around with a pinched expression and shook her head again.

Feeling guilty about Amity's hands and sorry for everything else she had suffered these past weeks, Paxton declared, "No one will tease you from now on. I won't let them."

Maybe she believed him or just needed to tell someone because Amity finally blurted out, "I think it was Princess Fee Fee, but I'm not sure."

"Princess who...?"

Looking horrified, Amity groaned and said, "Princess Fee Fee. It's what I call my bossy roommate, now tentmate. It was probably her or one of her little pets."

Scratching his head, Paxton asked, "Do you mean Felicia?"

Amity sighed. "Yes, the one and only."

"So, you do name-calling too?" Paxton said in a mock-accusing way.

"Only in my head. I would never embarrass anyone on purpose by making fun of them that way."

Paxton grimaced. Oh, that one had stung. But she was right. Even if he hadn't meant for the name-calling to do any harm, it still had. Well, he'd meant what he said. He wouldn't allow the others to tease her any further. And, he'd do his best to help too. The part he wasn't looking forward to was helping with the kids, but he was looking forward to spending more time with her.

Amity stumbled, and Paxton, mindful of her hands, grabbed her under the elbow to steady her. "Are you alright?" he asked.

Amity hesitated, then sighed again. "Yes, thank you." Then, a few steps later, she muttered, "Hedgehog."

"Who's a hedgehog?" Paxton asked as they continued trudging up the road.

"You are," said Amity without looking at him.

"Why am I a hedgehog?" Paxton asked incredulously, while kind of liking the sound of it. "Aren't they considered kind of cute?"

Amity turned his way, eyes glinting. "Sure, until they feel threatened. Then they curl up into a ball and get all spiky."

"Is that how you see me?"

"Yes!" Amity exclaimed with a smirk.

"I think you've spent a lot of time thinking about this."

"I have," she said. Her smile broadened. "But, of course, I think about a lot of things." They were both walking slowly now. And, as Amity spoke, a few children overtook them.

Chuckling a little, Paxton decided he liked the idea of Amity thinking of him. This side of her, where she teased back, was a lot of fun. He could maybe get to like it.

They continued in silence until a little boy trotted up and tugged on Amity's dress. Once he had her attention, he began chattering away about some exciting happenings. She was responding with "ohs, hmms, and reallys." *How could Amity understand any of this baby talk?* Soon, they were surrounded by a little cluster of children ranging in age from about three to possibly six or seven.

Sucking in a loud breath and wincing, Amity held her arms up and away from their excited little grabbing hands. Paxton quickly came to her rescue, setting himself between her and the exuberant children. "Hey! Hey! Everyone, listen here!" Paxton raised his voice to be heard over their excited chatter. Once he had their attention and they quieted down, he motioned to Amity's bandaged hands. "See, Amity's hands are hurt, so we can't touch them, or they will be hurt more." Collectively the children said, "Ohhh," and immediately stopped trying to hold her hands.

Amity threw a grateful glance his way. It felt good to have her approval. Amity was a different kind of girl, and she made him feel different too, protective maybe. He wasn't sure exactly.

Paxton rubbed his chest. Strangely that burning pain he'd felt earlier boring through him was gone. It was replaced with something else. It wasn't happiness, but he didn't know what it was exactly. Just maybe, it felt like hope.

Epilogue
Amity

THE BEDRAGGLED REFUGEES had been traveling through Penthia for just over two weeks when they finally crested the top of yet another hill. Forgotten was the endless stretch of road she'd walked as Amity gazed upon the grandest building she'd ever seen. Nothing could have prepared her for the splendor of the Temple of Riaas in Penthia. It stood in all its majesty upon a rounded ridge gently rising from the valley floor. The road leading to it was bordered by clusters of palm trees. The gleaming white temple had columns and spires reaching up toward the brilliant blue sky, but she couldn't observe any details of carvings or materials from this distance.

The already road-weary travelers had been struggling for the past few weeks as their journey east had turned southward. It was now the end of summer, and the unaccustomed heat and humidity were sometimes nearly unbearable. Amity wiped the sweat from her forehead and upper lip for the hundredth time that day and took a swallow from her water bottle. So this was to be her new home. It was beautiful but so different! She hoped it wasn't hot like this all year round, but if it was, she would just have to adjust. Sighing, she hung her water bottle back onto her belt.

Once settled in, she'd be able to write home. Amity badly wanted to receive news and especially hear about Esme's wedding. She also wanted to let her family know she was alright and had made it safely to Penthia. But, of course, she had no way of knowing that the borders of Livania were being closed and that she would never receive another letter from her family.

Amity didn't regret making the journey, even though she'd had more adventure in her almost fourteen years than she could have ever imagined or that she'd ever wanted. If she'd stayed behind, she'd have given up her dream in exchange for something safe and probably mundane. She didn't want "safe" and "mundane," and now she had Paxton in her life. She had fallen in love with him during the journey but hadn't told him so. For now, they were just good friends and companions. Occasionally, he still liked giving her a hard time, but she enjoyed the banter and teasing while holding her own with him. He never bullied her, and no one else had either after that day, way back in the Whistling Mountains.

True to his promise, Paxton had told the girls that he expected Amity's things returned to her by the following morning. No one was required to come forward as long as they returned her things. If not, he would bring the whole matter before the elders, and they would handle it. The prospect of having to confess everything they had been up to seemed to have been the motivation they needed because Amity was reunited with the precious gifts from Mama and Papa that very evening. She found her things waiting for her on her bedroll after she returned from having her hands seen to by Priestess Grace.

After they had crossed into the Kingdom of Penthia, the ordained from both temples had exchanged numerous letters. The refugees from Livania had known through words given by Riaas that they would be welcomed with open arms, but having the details in writing had been comforting. The Penthian temple would feed them and place them in temporary housing, during which time new wooden buildings would be erected to create a separate enclave for those from the Temple of Tilmar. It had been decided that they would remain their own order, so there was no need for them to assimilate into the Penthian clergy. Perhaps they would, in the future, or they might build their own temple.

"It's pretty amazing, isn't it?" Paxton asked as he came up to stand beside Amity. They gazed at the temple in the distance together.

Overwhelmed by the moment and unable to grasp it all, she whispered, "Yes, it is!"

People were resting at the top of the hill, catching their breath. They took in the view and pointed details out to one another and the children.

Someone at the temple had been watching for them because a delegation of people wearing white robes and darker uniforms came out of the main temple doors. They waved as they began walking along the road.

The tired refugees quickly gathered their belongings with renewed enthusiasm. They waved back as they made their way into the little valley to meet them.

A small group of excited children began to run and cheer, hopping up and down in front of the main group. The air of pure happiness and excitement was contagious, and within minutes, everyone around Amity began whooping and cheering too. She noticed more than a few dabbing at their eyes and felt her own begin to well up.

Suddenly, Paxton lifted Amity off her feet and swung her around in his arms. He whooped for joy along with everyone else. Laughter bubbled from Amity's lips, and happy tears spilled down her flushed cheeks.

After setting her back down on her feet, Paxton unexpectedly leaned close to her face. Then, without any warning, he kissed her full on the mouth! If Amity hadn't been so stunned, she would have returned the kiss. She was quite disappointed that she hadn't gathered her scattered wits quickly enough. She never expected a boy's lips could be so warm and soft. And it was over so quickly!

Amity touched her lips, looked at Paxton with wide eyes, and gave him a shy smile. He laughed and took her hand. And that's how they walked down the road toward their future. Together. Hand in hand.

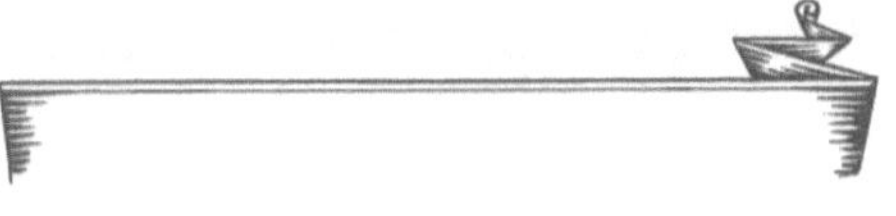

Epilogue
Anwen

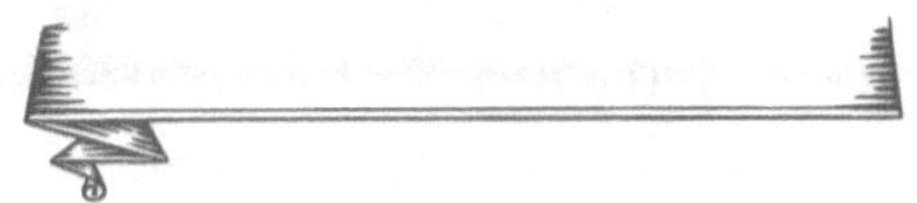

To all who have read this true account of recent events, may you consider a future where Livania reopens its borders, makes restitution with its neighbors where possible, and reinstates the Servants of Riaas at the temple in Tilmar.

With future hope,

Anwen, Queen of Livania

ANWEN SET DOWN HER favorite quill pen and blotted the final page before closing the journal. She stretched and gave a satisfied sigh. Geraint had known how important this project was to her and how terribly frustrated she'd been when she couldn't find time to do anything about it. Six months ago, when he'd found out that she was expecting their second child, he'd gifted her the pen, made of a golden feather from the rare sweeping eagle, and a beautiful dark-blue leather journal with gilt-edged vellum pages.

He'd smiled at her and said, "You'll be slowing down soon with public appearances and eventually stopping them completely until after the baby is born. Use that time to do what you've wanted to do this past year as queen. Write that book for future rulers."

It was the best present anyone had ever given her.

Geraint had turned out to be such a thoughtful man. He'd been right by her side since the moment of their betrothal. Somehow, she still couldn't imagine how, he'd convinced Father that being seen together in public would give the people a boost to their morale. The captain and the general had agreed with

Geraint and backed him. Their support might have been what actually swayed Father as he was always ready to listen to the opinions of military men over anyone else. Shortly after her betrothal, she also had her official inauguration and was finally recognized as the Crown Princess of Livania. The ceremony had been held during the Midsummer festivities, and then at the end of autumn, there had been a big wedding.

Anwen pushed away from the elegantly carved cherry wood desk and stood while clutching the corner of the desk for balance. She looked out the open balcony doors, enjoying the spectacular view and the early evening breeze on this beautiful summer day. Anwen was in the private study of the new wing that Father had begun building six years ago during that terrible spring of grief and slaughter. It was one of the few good things to come out of that time and a significant improvement on the old family quarters. The design provided suites for the royal family, rooms for the servants, and solar with an open-plan dining and sitting room. The L-shaped wing had taken four years to build, longer than planned, but the project had been competing with the new city walls and gates for manpower and resources. Considering how often the Walled City project had taken precedence, it was a wonder it had ever been finished.

Much of the Walled City was now complete, giving the people the safety and security they needed after small parties of Barinians and Karpydosans had begun invading and killing Livanians in retaliation. Father had been shocked to discover that Livanians were no longer welcome outside their borders and doubly shocked when their defenses were so easily breached by those seeking revenge. Anwen "hmmed" at the memory. She could almost laugh at how delusional he'd been, but it was no laughing matter. Father had gone into a rage when the first raiding parties had struck, causing him to suffer a debilitating attack. The royal healer was on hand to quickly attend to him. Thankfully, the raids had never been frequent and now seemed to be petering out altogether.

Anwen picked up the journal from the desk that had once been in Father's old sitting room. He'd been in his new chambers for less than a year when he'd suddenly passed away during the night. Father might not have died right then if he hadn't been sleeping alone, not when a royal healer was close at hand. But his increasing paranoia had caused him to put Mother in a separate suite, so he was only discovered the following morning when Roger, his manservant, had arrived to open his curtains. By then, it was too late to save him.

At least Anwen hadn't needed to move Mother out of the royal suite after she'd been crowned queen. Mother had stayed in her small domain, happy to be in her own space, no longer in the limelight. She'd never wanted to rule, always having been content to be Queen Consort, Queen Mother, and now Queen Grandmama.

Anwen held the journal above her protruding belly. She probably shouldn't sit here again until after the baby was born. Her bump was getting too big to fit comfortably behind the desk. At seven months, she looked bigger than she had just before Edson was born, she thought ruefully and then smiled to herself. That busy little boy gave her and Geraint so much joy.

There was a knock at the door. "Come in!" Anwen called.

Beitris stepped into the private study from the bedroom and curtsied. "It's almost suppertime, Your Majesty."

"Thank you, Beitris."

Beitris glanced at the journal Anwen was holding and smiled. "Did you finish it?"

"Yes, I did," Anwen said, returning the smile.

"Oh, that's good. Mister Calen is waiting for you in the solar."

Earlier, Anwen had sent a note asking Calen, the elderly royal librarian, to come to the solar just before suppertime. Calen had been in service to the crown even before Anwen was born. He'd always been like a grandfather to her, happy that she loved books and encouraging her to study any subject that caught her fancy. She suspected that sometimes she'd tried his patience with her constant barrage of questions on multiple topics, ranging from history and geography to the raising of fancy songbirds and how to curtsy like a lady. He'd never dismissed her or acted like she was a nuisance, though she was sure she had been. Remembering the rather portly librarian attempting to curtsy "like a lady" still made her laugh. He'd known she was sometimes lonely and had indulged her. Now he was one of the few people she trusted implicitly.

Anwen wanted to give Calen the completed journal for safekeeping, knowing he would never reveal its existence. "I hope he hasn't been waiting long," she said to Beitris, slightly concerned.

"No, not at all. He's having a cup of tea with Queen Lethe." Beitris walked to the balcony doors, latching them shut and drawing the curtains closed.

They left the darkened room and walked through the bedroom Anwen shared with her husband. She'd made a few changes to brighten it up when they moved in, but it hadn't required much work other than a thorough cleaning. It was a lovely room with high ceilings and the bonus of a balcony, the same balcony that stretched to her study.

Passing through the tall double doors, they came to a substantial L-shaped hallway around a spiral stone staircase. Beitris frowned at the relatively steep stairs. "I think it would be safer to go through the bathing chamber and use those stairs instead."

"Perhaps you're right. Geraint said the same thing to me this morning." Anwen was happy to have such caring people in her life. She was also in a good mood, having completed the journal. Someday, future kings and queens would learn the truth about King Arlo and the real reasons for their isolation from the rest of the world.

When her father was alive, he'd made sure everyone thought he was a big hero to Livania. He'd ordered parades and festivals and made sure that anyone who spoke out against him wasn't able to do so a second time. After his sudden death, her council of advisors had told her it was best to continue that story. They wanted to maintain the rather shaky stability they'd achieved after the last tumultuous years of King Arlo's reign. Initially, Anwen hadn't been happy with their advice and didn't want to comply, but remembering the words of Riaas from that horrifying trip to the cells convinced her to agree.

But she had no more need to worry. Calen would understand the importance of the journal and keep it safe. Furthermore, he would pass the secrets of his position on to his successor when the time came.

Instead of going down the spiral stairs, Anwen and Beitris turned left, passed Mother's door along the hallway, and entered the bathing room. A door at the other end of the room opened onto a passage with a staircase. The broad stone steps led down to the solar, then further down to the ground floor and passageway connecting the royal wing to the rest of the castle, where two or more guards kept watch to prevent unauthorized entry.

The two women made their way to the solar, where servants were busy setting the dining table for the evening meal. Supper had only recently become a private family affair for the royal family. They used to eat the midday and evening meals in the great hall. But Anwen had become increasingly uncomfortable sitting for extended periods as her pregnancy advanced, making it impossible to attend both. Concerned, Geraint had suggested they change their routine, making only one midday appearance in the dining hall each day, taking family dinners in the solar. Since the midday meal was much shorter and simpler, Anwen was able to stay for the whole meal. The change seemed to please everyone as the kitchen staff and servers had lighter work with dinner being less formal, and people who normally made an appearance could eat elsewhere.

Whenever Anwen felt stuck doing things simply because "that was the way they have always been done," Geraint would come up with a creative solution. She loved that about her husband. Overseeing the running of the kingdom kept them very busy. But this particular solution allowed them to eat together as a family in the evenings, kept her comfortable, and freed up some time for them both to dedicate to other things.

The servants quickly dropped a curtsy as Anwen passed them, heading toward the sitting area with Beitris following behind her. She could hear Calen's gruff voice saying something and then breaking into a chuckle accompanied by Mother's pleasant laughter. Jane, the mother of Beitris, was attending to them, pouring Mother another cup of tea and taking Calen's empty one.

As Anwen approached, Calen stood and bowed. "Good evening, Your Majesty. I hope you're well."

"Yes, I'm very well, thank you. And how are you, my old friend?"

She could barely see Calen's smile through his thick grey and ginger beard, but his bright blue eyes twinkled merrily under the bushy brows. "I'm also well, my dear. I hear you have something for me." His eyes looked briefly down at the journal she clasped to her breast.

"Yes, I do." Anwen hugged the book for a moment longer, then quickly held it out, proud to finally be able to show off her work. "These past few months, I've been working on this journal and just finished it today. Contained herein is a complete record of what really happened six years ago and how it changed our kingdom from what it was to what it is now."

Mother gasped, looking horrified by Anwen's statement.

Anwen ignored her and continued speaking, "I received eyewitness accounts from Captain Arten and others who participated in events as they unfolded. I read all the official military reports, and my husband assisted me whenever I needed more information."

Calen glanced at Lethe as she made a noise that sounded rather like a strangled squeak. He took the journal carefully in his wrinkled hands. "Hmm, an ambitious and important undertaking, indeed. And, now, what would you have me do with it?"

"I would ask you to keep it somewhere safe, along with instructions to pass it on to your successor. There will someday be kings or queens who will think about reopening our borders. They need to know the truth of our story so they can prepare accordingly."

Jane snatched Mother's teacup just before it hit the floor as Mother shakily got to her feet and demanded, "How could you do such a thing? This book will bring dishonor to your family name!"

Anwen took a deep breath before straightening her spine and replying, "Mother, I'm doing the honorable thing. I'm telling the truth."

"This is all so shameful! All of it! What's in the past should stay in the past," Mother said, flinging out her arm. "But instead, we'll be judged by future generations, and *nothing* will be forgotten. Don't you care about that?"

Anwen had been expecting Mother's disapproval, but she hadn't been prepared for the strength of her outburst. Before she could respond, Mother switched tactics. Reducing her volume but still sounding intensely agitated, she said, "Calen, don't tell me you approve of this!"

Calen took a few steps towards Mother and took one of her now shaking hands in his steady one. "My dear, Lethe. Do not be distressed. Telling the truth is always the best path to follow. Your brave daughter's duty as queen includes writing down history as it happens or assigning someone else to do it. Don't forget, she has had the help of the good captain, the king consort, and I'm sure others. I will also do my part."

"But—"

Anwen, hoping to prevent any other objections, interrupted her by saying, "Mother, you have nothing to fear. Calen will keep this history safe, and only in the distant future will this journal be read. I can only hope it has the impact I intend for it to have, but it will not be opened in your lifetime. Of that, I'm sure."

"But your father's actions—"

Anwen had had enough. "Father's choices were his own, as were everyone else's," she said sharply. "Many people died. I don't know what the people of the future will think, but I prefer they judge me on the truth rather than on some claptrap made up around a bonfire!"

Right then, little Edson came running through, unknowingly interrupting the mother-daughter standoff. "Mama, Mama!" he called while waving his floppy brown stuffed bunny. His soft toy was well-worn as it went everywhere he went.

Anwen bent down to hug her four-year-old son as he crashed into her legs. He was a beautiful child, having his father's green eyes and his mother's dark wavy hair. He was already too heavy to pick up, even before she'd found out she was pregnant. "Yes, sweetie. What is it?"

Edson held up his bunny and took a big breath, but then noticed the other adults watching him. His eyebrows drew down as his lips pressed together.

Calen smiled and bowed to the small boy. "Hello, Your Highness." Edson looked a little unsure, remaining silent until Calen added, "Hello, Bunny."

This made Edson smile. "Hello, Mister Calen," he said in a high-pitched voice, holding on tightly to his mother's side with one hand and Bunny with the other.

"Don't forget to greet your grandmama," reminded Anwen in a stage whisper.

"Hi, Gran'mama!" Edson twisted around his mother's legs and giggled.

Lethe sat down in her chair, reaching toward her grandson. Edson let go of his mother and ran into his grandmama's arms. He bent at the waist and pressed his head into her lap, squishing Bunny between them.

Seeing the open affection between the two always warmed Anwen's heart.

"Well, I'd best be going," said Calen. "I have a bit of work yet to complete today."

"Of course, and thank you," said Anwen.

"I should be thanking you." Calen held up the journal. "I promise to take good care of it."

Anwen smiled as Calen bowed to the three of them, turned, and left the room. Lethe looked over the top of Edson's head and frowned, indicating that she was planning on continuing this discussion later. Anwen used to fear those frowns, as she had never been allowed to stand up to her mother. Knowing that she could, made her feel giddy at times.

As Calen was going out, Geraint strolled in, and the two men greeted each other warmly.

Anwen's smile grew as she watched her husband approaching. The servants paused in their preparations to bow as he passed by them and then returned to their work. The last six years had been kind to Geraint, and he was more handsome than ever. He also looked very stylish these days. Her father's very talented manservant, Roger, had transferred into Geraint's service upon his death. While Anwen thought Roger was sometimes a little too fond of puffs and flourishes, his tailoring couldn't be faulted. In fact, she was considering asking him to alter a few of the things in her wardrobe—

"Hello, my dear one," Geraint said, interrupting her thoughts. He took her by the shoulders and gave her a soft kiss on the lips. Turning to Lethe, he added, "And, hello, Mother." He stepped over to his mother-in-law, bent down, and kissed her cheek.

Both women flashed genuine smiles, as did their maids, captured by his charm.

Looking down at his son, Geraint asked, "Did you tell them what we did today?"

Edson lifted his head from his grandmama's lap and said, "Oh, let me! Let me tell!"

"Well, go ahead then." Geraint smiled and motioned with his hand.

Anwen lowered herself onto a cushioned seat, preparing to listen, as Edson went to stand beside his father. Anwen was amazed at how tall he was getting. He nearly reached the height of his father's belt.

Edson said in an excited rush, "We went to the stables, and Lenart showed us my foal! I'm going to have my own horse, just like Dusk. And Lenart said that I can name her!"

Eyes widening in genuine surprise, Anwen asked, "What do you mean, your foal?"

"Papa, tell her! Tell her!" Edson said, tugging on his father's tunic.

Chuckling, Geraint said, "The colt is Dusk's most recent foal, a real beauty, and the spitting image of her sire." Geraint looked down at Edson and ruffled his son's hair. "She's going to be yours, but she needs to grow up before she'll be able to carry you around. You'll need to work on your horsemanship and be a little taller."

Edson bounced up and down and said, "But I can already ride!"

"Yes, but riding Blackie isn't the same as riding a young horse will be. Blackie knows everything and helps you learn. Your filly won't know very much, and you'll have to help her to learn what to do. Do you remember what Lenart said?"

"I can start to ride her a little when I'm seven?"

Geraint nodded. "And?"

A crease formed on Edson's forehead as he tried to remember. "I must practice by caring for Blackie every day."

Lenart insisted that everyone, even the royal family, learn not just to ride but to care for their own horses and clean their own tack. No one was allowed to merely toss the reins to the stable hands when they returned from a ride, as he felt the work fostered respect for both the horses and the hands. Much to the surprise of visitors to the castle stables, even Queen Anwen picked out feet and brushed her own horse.

Geraint's tone sobered as he continued, "That's right. Caring for a horse takes hard work. You'll need to prove you can do that. And, in all that time, you can visit your filly every day so she gets to know you really well."

Edson turned and beamed. "You see, Mama! It's true."

"I see." Anwen pursed her lips, not completely sold on the idea of Edson riding anything other than solid dependable old Blackie. Seeing Edson's hopeful expression, she decided she had several years to negotiate the question. "Do you have a name for her yet?"

Edson smiled and said, "Lenart wants me to think of lots of names and try them out before I decide."

"That's good advice," Anwen said, mouth quirking. "You wouldn't want to choose the wrong one."

The servants began bringing trays and bowls of food to the dining table. The smell of savory vegetable soup and roasted meat reached Anwen's nose. Her mouth watered, and her stomach felt like it was trying to eat itself. She hadn't realized how hungry she was.

While Lethe and Edson made their way to the table, Geraint helped Anwen to her feet. "I saw Calen was carrying your journal," he said close to her ear. "What was your mother's reaction?"

"She wasn't pleased," Anwen said with a grimace.

"I'm sure she wasn't." Geraint squeezed her waist. "You know, I'm so very proud of you."

Smiling, Anwen replied, "Yes. I know."

Geraint gently tapped her round belly. "I wonder if this little one will be a girl. If she is, I bet she'll be just as amazing as her mother." Anwen laughed softly, and Geraint kissed her cheek. "I love it when you laugh."

She laughed again and squeezed his arm. "By the way, how tall is this filly likely to get? Age seven is a little young to be riding something the size of Dusk. I'd feel better knowing she was going to be quite a bit smaller than he is."

"She is meant to be his first horse-sized horse," Geraint replied.

Anwen raised her eyebrows and tried to look stern but was unsuccessful.

"I think she'll be a perfect size," Geraint said with a wink, drawing Anwen to his side, and she gave a smile in response. He linked arms with her, and together they walked arm-in-arm to eat supper with little Edson and Lethe.

From the Author

DID YOU ENJOY THIS book? Please tell others and leave a short review, what you liked about the story and how it made you feel. Reviews and word-of-mouth make it possible for others to find my books so I can keep writing stories. I love hearing from my readers. I also have links at the end of the book so you can follow me and keep in touch. Thank you!

GLOSSARY

SERVANTS OF RIAAS

Amity – a novice at the Temple of Riaas

Riaas the Watcher – their god

Esme – Amity's oldest sister

Felicia – Amity's roommate

Eva – a novice

Dante – High Priest

Celeste – High Priestess

Paxton – the grandson of Dante and Celeste

Prudence – Paxton's mother

Henry – Paxton's roommate

Sereen – a novice

Laree – a novice

Hileon – a novice

Jerome – a priest

Justin – a priest

Grace – a priestess

ROYALS

Arlo – King of Livania

Lethe – Queen of Livania

Edson – Crown Prince of Livania

Anwen – Princess of Livania

Geraint – Lord of Elmsbridge

Edson – a young prince

Marin – King of Karpydosa
Jurem – Crown Prince of Karpydosa
Rose – Princess of Karpydosa
Lily – Princess of Karpydosa
Tarson – King of Bariny

OTHERS

Isla – a chicken farmer
Silas – retired manservant to King Arlo
Roger – new manservant to King Arlo
Lenart – Head Stableman
Glen – a guard, Lenart's son
Jake – a guard
Arten – Captain of the King's Guard
Balcom – Commander of the King's Army
Dur – a merchant
Finis – a merchant
Tom – a farmer
Joan – a farmer
Jane – maid to Queen Lethe
Beitris – maid to Princess Anwen
Calen – Royal Librarian

HORSES

Darkness – King Arlo's black stallion
Dusk – Lord Geraint's blue-roan stallion
Cobble – Lord Geraint's chunky bay gelding
Blackie – Farmer Tom's sturdy black pony

THE Princess
WAYFINDERS BOOK 2
(Sample Reading)

C.A. MORLEY

Chapter 1
Myra (abridged)

THE STACCATO TAP-TAPPING of Myra's leather-soled shoes on the slightly uneven flagstones kept time with the rapid beating of her heart. It was a long walk from the stillroom cellar door up to the solar, especially if going by way of the castle courtyard. And today, she wanted this walk to last for, perhaps, a month... or even two. Although she desperately wanted to delay the upcoming confrontation, she still walked quickly. What she didn't need was to get into bigger trouble for deliberately keeping her sister waiting.

At least Nula had summoned her to their private solar, not into the great hall in front of the entire court. Myra couldn't bear to face an audience, not now that she'd been caught breaking the law. Hopefully, she could talk her way around whatever had been reported.

Realizing her steps had slowed, Myra picked up the pace. Nula had very little patience these days.

Myra hurried past two merchants deep in discussion. She grimaced slightly, hoping they hadn't noticed her lack of composure. Ladies in Livania were "always to look serene," but sometimes Myra found the task impossible. Just another thing on her list of failings. Well, she supposed, it was a relatively small one.

The life of a princess held many duties and responsibilities, but Myra's had increased in the last year since her sister became the queen. It was an unexpected change and a shock to both of them, but no one could have anticipated the accident that took their parents' lives. Receiving the crown, hard on the heels of the memorial, had made her sister more of a perfectionist than ever before. Queen Nula cared a lot about her own duties, expected Myra to fulfill hers perfectly, and was a stickler when it came to things she considered "principles." Sometimes Myra just wanted to chuck the whole thing and become a milkmaid. Well, maybe not a milkmaid, but something more ordinary anyway.

Myra looked up at the simple stone facade towering above her and thought of a line she'd seen in one of her brother's books. "The people, the policies, and the palace haven't changed much these past three hundred years." *Hmm. That does have a nice ring to it.* If only it were an actual palace instead of just a big plain castle, then living inside its walls might have felt more romantic. But her home was a fortress first, and she doubted it had ever been what you'd call cozy. One of Myra's least favorite tutors, who'd only ever droned on in monotones, always said, "It was built on fortitude and maintained with diligence." *Gah!*

Pausing in front of the huge oak door that led inside, Myra smoothed her hair and quickly retied the single braid that hung over her right shoulder. A guard cleared his throat, and Myra blinked. How long had he been holding the door for her? Myra lifted her chin, nodded to the guard, and entered with purposeful steps.

She'd never set out to break the law, but her *intent* wasn't going to matter. The cold hard fact was that she had. Oh, but getting swept up in Berne's whirling energy was like being drunk on life!

Myra never felt so happy and free as she did out in the woods, foraging for plants for the stillroom. Since meeting Berne on one of those outings, Myra felt even happier. And despite the secrecy around their meetings, she'd discovered an even more satisfying freedom when talking to him.

During one of their first conversations, Berne had confided that he was from the Kingdom of Fulsan, a wild and savage country located northeast of Livania. He spoke almost perfect Livanian, and Myra found his rumbling accent different and compelling. They'd spoken for hours on so many different topics, and he seemed to really listen to everything she said. He was so interesting, not boring or predictable like *everyone else* she knew!

Myra missed Berne desperately. If only she didn't have to live two lives, snatching moments with him in secret. She had, of course, withheld her true identity from him, pretending to be of common birth and of no import. He'd been so quick to believe her when she'd said she worked for an herbalist in the Walled City that she began feeling a little smug at how easily she'd fooled him. But Myra liked not being "The Princess" around him. It allowed her the opportunity to be someone different, and it was *so* romantic!

As she made her way down the corridor, an unexplained uneasiness suddenly overcame her. Myra pressed her hands to the necklace hidden under her tunic, safely tucked away from prying eyes. It felt reassuring as if she were holding Berne's strong, warm hand to her heart. Myra just wanted to hold onto him forever and never let go.

After getting to know each other a bit, Berne had given Myra the necklace. A tiny silver charm engraved with a wing was attached to a thinly plaited leather cord. Dangling on either side was a small feather from the neck of a sweeping eagle. He'd told her that sweeping eagles often nested in the deep forests along the mountains above his home. He'd chuckled and added that he saw them fairly often.

As he hung the cord around her neck, Berne had told her he'd made the necklace especially for her. She treasured it and had not taken it off since, except while bathing. It was beautiful and unusual. Just as rare as he was. It spoke to her of wildness and freedom. The huge eagles were so rare and elusive that some considered them a myth. Now Myra knew, for sure, they weren't a myth, even if she couldn't tell anyone.

The feathers were streaked golden-yellow and glimmered like honey, darkening to black tips, the same coloring as Berne's hair. He told her the coloring was common to the Oskari people, only sometimes darker or lighter. She'd known there were tribes in Fulsan, but no specifics. The people used to be as reclusive as Livanians, but things were changing.

Berne had asked Myra many questions about Livanians, their customs, and her day-to-day life, and she'd spoken freely on what she considered "safe" topics. Myra had used her fictitiously low status to claim ignorance of the doings of the nobility, and she was positive that her masquerade had been flawless.

It might feel like a long time ago, but it had only been that morning when Myra and Berne had last seen each other. While sharing a passionate kiss, they were interrupted by a crashing noise in the underbrush. Leaping to their feet, they saw an indistinct figure disappearing through the trees. Most likely, it had been a forester going about his daily business, spotting them purely by chance. *Such bad luck!* Afraid that he'd run off to alert the scouts, Myra and Berne had fled in opposite directions. One of the armed scouts on patrol in the forest would've confronted them instead of running off, and Myra supposed that could have ended very badly. At least this way, there was a good chance that Berne had escaped.

When Myra had curiously asked Berne how he avoided the scouts patrolling the woodlands and farmlands of Livania, he had winked at her and said he was extra stealthy. Myra knew Berne wasn't being completely truthful but didn't pursue the subject. Maybe he had a secret or two, but then again, so did she.

Myra approached the passage to the L-shaped royal wing with apprehension. Guards always kept an alert watch at the base of the private staircase. Not wanting to give them anything more to gossip over than what they might know already, Myra controlled her breathing, pulled her shoulders back, and moved with as much grace as she could muster. It took a lot out of her to create a nonchalant façade. As soon as she was out of sight, it crumbled.

She scrambled up the broad stone steps leading to the first and second floors. The short climb left her breathless and uncomfortably warm, but now a chill went through her. What Myra didn't need, and was trying to avoid at all costs, was to have the accusation of "fornicator" added to her list of crimes. Though frowned upon among the common folk, such an accusation among the nobility could make her completely unmarriageable. The perceived lack of self-discipline would mark her as untrustworthy.

Myra shivered as she realized just how bad things could get. Her time of the month was late – not so unusual – but six weeks ago, she'd given herself fully to Berne in a moment of unbridled passion. The tips of her ears grew hot. What if? Her legs felt weak, and she wobbled. After giving herself a mental shake, she locked that thread of thought away to examine later.

The tall double doors of the first floor opened directly into the solar, a large dining and sitting room divided by stone columns. Myra was relieved to see that she had arrived ahead of Nula. Her sister was always busy with queenly duties and frequently ran a little behind schedule. Everyone understood they were to wait for the queen and never the other way around.

Since their parents' deaths, Nula never seemed to stop working. In fact, she never seemed to relax or stop frowning. Myra's own brow wrinkled as she tried to remember the last time they'd shared a lighthearted moment. Myra grieved the loss of their parents every day, but sometimes she felt she'd lost her sister too.

Using the moment afforded her, Myra stood inside the dining area on the dark-stained wooden floor to catch her breath while enjoying the room's coolness. High-arched windows along the south wall allowed in the mountain breeze, making the room one of the most comfortable in the castle.

Myra made her way towards the sitting room end of the solar, passing the polished oak wood dining table with its leather upholstered chairs and fragrant floral centerpiece. Between the dining and sitting room areas were two woven rugs with a huge stone fireplace against the south wall, which stood cold and empty.

Warm walnut wood covered the ceiling. Eleven years ago, Father had had the old stone ceiling remodeled with curved beams and decorative woodwork painted with accents of red, green, and yellow. Both parents were now gone, and those colors had faded.

The woodwork had been Father's gift to Mother on their twelfth anniversary. Myra had been five and could still remember it vividly. Every night, they would climb onto their big brother's large bed where Mother would read to them since the sitting room was temporarily unavailable. After the new ceiling was completed, Myra spent many happy evenings gazing at the colors and patterns while Mother read, but deep down, she'd loved snuggling on the bed with her siblings even more.

In the sitting room were another two rugs as well as two large bookcases, which held personal selections from each family member and a few decorative items. Their brother, Adrian, had gone missing two years ago, but his books were still on the oak shelves where he'd left them. It was the same when their parents died. Myra would sometimes read their books, wanting to bring the memory of them closer. Nula didn't like reminiscing with her about their brother or their parents, which made her grief harder to bear.

Even though Berne could never replace those she'd lost, Myra was starting to feel whole again. She still wore the linen tunic over linen trousers from that morning in the woods when their kiss was cut short. It was a practical outfit for riding, but she had also taken time with her appearance, having Berne in mind. The tunic was her favorite color, aquamarine, with a round neckline and embroidered trim. Her eyes weren't opalescent and striking like Nula's, so

Mother used to encourage her to wear shades of blue to enhance their color. She felt rewarded as Berne had commented on how much he liked her sky-blue eyes, which were very different from his amber.

When Myra remembered why she was in the solar, her happy mood soured. The urgent summons probably meant the end of her trysts with Berne. Myra nervously played with her braid, not daring to sit down. She didn't want to give the impression she wasn't taking things seriously.

On a round table was a pitcher of water. She quickly poured a glass and drank deeply, quenching her sudden thirst. Just as she set the glass down, Nula entered. Myra straightened and her stomach churned.

Nula walked with precise steps. The sound of her heels clicking against the wooden floor heightened Myra's tension. As Nula stepped across the woven rugs in the middle of the room, the nail-biting sound was swallowed up, but Myra's stomach still churned. Drinking all that water hadn't helped.

Her sister was particularly stunning today in a flowing purple gown with embroidered trim and a midnight-blue sash tied at the waist. A portion of her pale-blonde hair was braided in a circle around her head, while the rest flowed loosely down her back. She wore a simple gold circlet with a vibrant white opal at the center. The opal was an important symbol of their kingdom, representing those, like Nula, with opalescent eyes.

As Nula passed by, the perfume of lavender and lemons gently permeated the room. It was a new summer fragrance and her sister's most recent favorite. Nula had only half a head's height on Myra, but today she appeared almost to loom over her and seemed more regal. Myra wasn't expected to curtsy when they were in private, but this time, she felt compelled to.

Nula was only two years older but treated Myra like she was still a child. Myra tried not to hold it against her. Becoming Queen of Livania was a huge responsibility, and nothing could have prepared her to rule just a year ago at seventeen. Even though Nula had people to advise her, no one could replace Father. She was doing her best.

Thankfully, Myra wasn't burdened with being the queen.

Nula briskly sat on her cushioned chair, facing Myra. Her posture was ramrod straight, her chin held high, and her hands planted flat on the armrests of the heavy oak chair. She looked Myra up and down, mouth pinched.

Even though they were sisters, they were two very different people. Today was no exception.

Clasping her hands to prevent them from shaking, Myra endured her sister's silence. It was as much punishment as when she spoke. Three minutes under Nula's flinty gaze felt like thirty. It was worse when her eyes flashed colored light. Livanians born with eyes the color of iridescent white opals had the gift of healing. Their eyes dulled or brightened depending on their mood. Mother had once had opal eyes too. Myra would have preferred her firm chastising to Nula's fiery anger, and she missed their mother more than ever. Nula didn't have Mother's restraint, and her anger could quickly spike.

Sweat trickled down Myra's forehead and moisture beaded on her upper lip, but she dared not lick it away or fidget under her sister's stony gaze. Even though they were sisters, Nula was queen, and Myra's life was in her hands.

"Myra, you were seen with an outsider. The report I heard is you were very familiar with this individual. Explain yourself."

Briefly, Myra closed her eyes, composing her thoughts. There was no use trying to lie, but she wouldn't tell her sister everything. Perhaps she could convince her sister to give love a chance. She lifted her chin and squared her shoulders. "Your information is correct, My Queen."

Nula scowled. "I gave you the freedom to enter the woods, knowing how much it meant to you, and trusting our scouts to keep you safe. But you've broken my trust." Nula's fingers gripped the armrests. "If news of this gets out, I'll have no choice but to charge you with treason."

"But you're the queen!"

"Exactly, Myra. I cannot be seen as playing favorites. People won't stand for it. Do you realize you'll face death or imprisonment? And I'll be the one forced to pass judgment on you."

Myra cringed, wishing she could block her ears. She'd hoped for the best. She wasn't prepared to deal with the worst.

"Thankfully, the man who saw the two of you together came straight to me, and I commanded my guards not to tell anyone. How could you place both of us in such a terrible position?"

That made Myra flinch. Oh, she felt wretched. She never meant to hurt her sister. "I'm sorry."

As if not hearing Myra's apology, Nula continued, "And all for an outsider!"

"But—"

"I want to know exactly what's going on. No more secrets. Who were you seeing and how did he get past our scouts?"

This discussion was not going well. Digging her nails into her palms, she said, "His name is Berne."

"Burn? Like fire?"

A snort escaped Myra from tightly spun emotions. "I asked him the same thing. It's spelled B-E-R-N-E." She took a deep breath and added, "I don't know how he got past the scouts. He never explained."

"That didn't worry you?"

"Well, maybe at first, but once I got to know him, I realized he's a good man."

"Go ahead, enlighten me."

Myra flinched at Nula's antagonistic tone. "He's thoughtful and charming, and—"

"How do you know he wasn't just putting on an act to win your trust? Hmm?" Nula motioned with her hand. "Where is he from? What does he want?"

Clasping her forearms in frustration, Myra replied, "He is from the Kingdom of Fulsan. He mentioned having to attend a family meeting, but where they live exactly, I don't know."

"What did you talk about then?"

"I'm trying to explain. Just..." She blinked a few times, holding back tears. "He's an outdoors kind of man, and he knows his plants. He's seen our walled city from a distance but never lived in one and wondered what that was like. And, we talked a lot about me."

Nula's eyes flashed, and she sat forward. "You gave him information about our people and the royal family? I thought you were smarter!"

"No, no! I didn't tell him anything about us, not at all. I didn't even let him know I was a princess. I was careful, I promise!"

"Well, you won't be seeing him anymore and that's final."

"You can't! I need to see him again!" Myra didn't like sounding desperate, but she was. Berne had revived her soul and given her heart wings to fly. If he was taken from her, she'd be crushed.

Nula's eyes widened and her nostrils flared. "Why this big need? How long have you known him?"

"Just four months, but it's long enough to know he means everything to me and—"

"Why are you risking our way of life for some... *outsider*?"

"He is not just some... *outsider*," Myra said, mimicking Nula's derisive tone. "You would understand if you were in love."

"If I was in love? How can you even say you're in love after only a few short months? Regardless, even if I did fall in love, it would never be with an outsider." Nula took a few breaths. "I forbid you to have further contact with him."

Tears sprang to Myra's eyes. "You can't! I need to see him."

"Again, you do not *need* to see him. What nonsense."

"It's not nonsense. When I'm with him, I feel happy, and all is right in the world." Myra kneeled and reached for her sister's hands, stopping short of touching her. Before Nula was queen, and the wall of formality had risen between them, Myra would've held her sister's hands without hesitation. So much had changed in such a short amount of time.

Nula leaned forward and clasped Myra's hands. "I have to do what's best for the kingdom, and you should too."

Myra's mouth was dry, making it impossible to swallow. "I can't," she whispered.

Nula let go of her hands and sat up, lengthening her spine. "Trust me, you will get over him. Life will go on."

There was no use arguing with her sister. Life didn't just go on when the love of your life wasn't allowed to be part of it.

Nula had put up walls around her heart that were higher than those around the city and castle. Livanians insisted on staying behind walls. The walls were a constant reminder of the Great Betrayal. It was three hundred years ago, but people still discussed it as if it had happened yesterday. Myra didn't like living in the past, nursing old wounds, and she refused to dwell on the subject. Of course, she felt terrible that Livania's crown prince had been murdered all those years ago. That awful betrayal had brought a dark time for their people, but she didn't believe this endless, self-imposed isolation was good for their kingdom. This was one topic Nula refused to discuss.

Myra stood and shook her head.

Nula's eyes narrowed. "You've placed me in an untenable position, Myra. Please, don't force me to choose between my sister and my kingdom."

Myra nodded. "Yes, My Queen." There was nothing more either of them could say or do. Livanians were stuck in their ways, and there was no changing that.

Nula stood, ending the discussion. She shook out her dress as if shaking off something unpleasant, but when she walked out, her steps were less poised than they had been upon entering.

Myra was left alone in the solar. She didn't like being alone, but this was becoming her new normal. True friends were almost impossible to find when you were of royal blood. She was used to that and accepted it. Family was better than friends. Family was everything. Now Myra's family was almost nonexistent.

Berne said he'd be away for two weeks at an important family meeting. What was his family like? Would they open their hearts to her in a way her family refused to for him? Could she leave Livania and take that chance? She wasn't sure, but she had time to think over her next move. Maybe a future with Berne in the wide-open world would be better than a lonely future behind Livania's walls.

Her sister preferred living separately from the rest of the world, but Myra needed more. And it was clear that remaining a princess of Livania meant imprisonment, maybe literally, for the rest of her life.

She sighed.

Nula could keep her walls. Myra had a life to live.

ABOUT THE AUTHOR

WHEN C.A. MORLEY ISN'T reading about relatable characters in magical places, she's writing about them in her epic romantic fantasy series, Wayfinders. By no means an adrenaline junky, multiple interests and a fearless spirit have led her to experience new things with abandon, making her feel like she's lived at least three lives. Having visited over forty countries, some of her more memorable adventures include wandering desert roads below the carved sandstone cliffs of Petra, along lava-stone lanes in ancient Pompeii, and on cobblestone streets in medieval Prague. An American wife and mother of four, she resides in the scenic wine region of South Africa.

You can follow C.A. Morley by visiting her website at
www.camorleyauthor.com

Don't miss out!

Visit the website below and you can sign up to receive emails whenever C.A. Morley publishes a new book. There's no charge and no obligation.

https://books2read.com/r/B-A-GZFV-KVNBC

BOOKS2READ

Connecting independent readers to independent writers.

9 798987 079706